Benson John Lossing, Anna Seward

The Two Spies

Nathan Hale and John André

Benson John Lossing, Anna Seward

The Two Spies
Nathan Hale and John André

ISBN/EAN: 9783337398798

Printed in Europe, USA, Canada, Australia, Japan

Cover: Foto ©Andreas Hilbeck / pixelio.de

More available books at **www.hansebooks.com**

NATHAN HALE AND JOHN ANDRÉ

BY

BENSON J. LOSSING, LL. D.

ILLUSTRATED WITH PEN-AND-INK SKETCHES BY H. ROSA

ANNA SEWARD'S MONODY ON MAJOR ANDRÉ

NEW YORK
D. APPLETON AND COMPANY
I, 3, AND 5 BOND STREET
1886

FORETALK.

THIS little volume contains a brief account of the most important events in the life-career of two notable spies in our War for Independence, NATHAN HALE and JOHN ANDRÉ. They were both young men, well educated, endowed with genius and ability for conspicuous achievements, brave and accomplished soldiers, pure and virtuous in private char-acter, truthful, manly, refined in thoughts and manners, hand-some in person, lovely in disposition, and beloved by all who knew them.

Yet they were spies!

" Spies," says Vattel, "are generally condemned to capi-tal punishment, and not unjustly, there being scarcely any other way of preventing the mischief which they may do. For this reason a man of honor, who would not expose himself to die by the hand of a common executioner, ever declines serving as a spy. He considers it beneath him, as it can seldom be done without some kind of treachery."

May not a spy be a man of lofty honor, and act under the inspiration of disinterested patriotism? Stratagem, an artifice or scheme for deceiving an enemy in war, is re-garded as honorable, but is it not seldom exercised " with-out some kind of treachery "?

It is the *motive* which gives true character to the deed. When the motive is a purely mercenary one, the deed is dishonorable; when it is the lofty one of a desire to serve one's country or his race, unselfishly, the act is certainly honorable. Nathan Hale truthfully said, "Every kind of service necessary for the public good becomes honorable by being necessary."]

The motives of the two spies were expressed by them-selves. (Hale said: "I wish to be useful. If the exigencies of my country demand a peculiar service, its claims to the performance of that service are imperious)" André avowed that in the enterprise in which he was engaged all he sought "was military glory, the applause of his king and country, and, perhaps, a brigadiership."

The last words uttered by André under the gibbet indicated that his supreme thought at that moment was of *him-self*. He said to the American officers present, "I request you, gentlemen, that you will bear me witness to the world that I die like a brave man." Hale's last words upon the ladder indicated that his supreme thought at that moment was of his *country*. He said, "I only regret that I have but one life to lose for my country!"

In 1856 a "Life of Captain Nathan Hale," by I. W. Stuart, was published at Hartford, in a small volume of 230 pages. In 1861 "The Life and Career of Major John André," by Winthrop Sargeant, was published at Boston in a small octavo volume of nearly 500 pages. It is an exhaustive work. To these two books I acknowledge much indebtedness.

The spirited pen-and-ink sketches which illustrate this little volume were largely copied from original drawings by the author; also from other original drawings and autographs. The two pictures, *Cunningham destroying Hale's Letters*, and *The Tournament*, are original designs by the artist.

This volume contains the full text of André's " Cow-Chase," and the famous " Monody on Major André," by Miss Anna Seward, with a portrait and a brief biographical sketch of the author ; also three characteristic letters written by André to Miss Seward, when he was a youth of eighteen. The " Monody," I believe, has never been published in America.

B. J. L.

THE RIDGE, *April, 1886.*

.

CONTENTS.

NATHAN HALE.

CHAPTER I.

CHAPTER II.

CHAPTER III.

JOHN ANDRÉ.

ILLUSTRATIONS.

NATHAN HALE.

HALE'S BIRTHPLACE.

CHAPTER I.

In a picturesque region of Tolland County, Connecticut, twenty miles eastward of Hartford, situated upon an emine, ce which commands a beautiful and extensive prospect westward toward the State capital, there once stood, and perhaps now stands, a pleasant farm-house, built of wood, an two stories in height.* In that house, on the 6th of June, 1755, a child was born whose name appears conspicuous in our national history. It was a boy, and one of twelve children, whose father, Richard Hale, had emigrated in early life from Newberry, in Massachusetts, to Coventry, and there married Elizabeth Strong, a charming maiden eighteen years of age. He was a descendant of Robert Hale, or Hales, who settled in Charlestown, in 1632, and who seems to have been a scion of the Hales of Kent, for he bore their coat-of-arms—three broad arrows feathered white, on a red field.

Both Richard and Elizabeth Hale were of the strictest sect of the Puritans of their day. They revered the Bible

* See the frontispiece, copied from a drawing by J. W. Barber, of New Haven, in 1: .o.

2

as the voice of God; reverenced magistrates and gospel ministers as his chosen servants; regarded the strict observance of the Christian Sabbath as a binding obligation, and family worship and grace before meals as imperative duties and precious privileges.)

The sixth child of Richard and Elizabeth Hale they named NATHAN. He was feeble in body at the beginning of his life, and gave very little promise of surviving the period of infancy; but tender motherly care carried him safely over the critical second year, and he became a robust child, physically and mentally. He grew up a lively, sweet-tempered, and beautiful youth; and these qualities marked his young manhood.

Nathan Hale, the distinguished person alluded to, bright and active, loved out-of-door pastimes, and communing with Nature everywhere. He was conspicuous among his companions for remarkable athletism. He would spring, with apparent ease, out of one hogshead into another, through a series; and he would place his hand upon a fence as high as his head, and spring over it at a bound with apparently little effort.

Having an intense thirst for knowledge, young Hale was very studious. His father designed him for the Christian ministry, and he was fitted for college by the Rev. Dr. Huntington, one of the most eminent Congregational divines and scholars of his day, and then the pastor of the parish in which Nathan was born.

Young Hale entered Yale College when in the sixteenth year of his age. His brother Enoch, the grandfather of Rev. Edward Everett Hale, of Boston, and two years the senior of Nathan, entered Yale at the same time. The students then numbered about sixty. His course of col-

lege-life was eminently praiseworthy; and he was gradu-
ated with the highest honors in September, 1773. Popular with all the students, the tutors, and the faculty, he
was always a welcome visitor in the best families of New
Haven.

In the autumn of 1848 I visited the venerable Eneas
Munson, M. D., at New Haven. He had been assistant surgeon, under Dr. Thatcher, in the old War for Independence.
He knew young Hale well during the later period of his life
at Yale College, for he was then a frequent visitor at the
home of Dr. Munson's father.

"I was greatly impressed," said Dr. Munson, "with
Hale's scientific knowledge, evinced during his conversation
with my father. I am sure he was equal to André in solid
acquirements, and his taste for art and talents as an artist
were quite remarkable. His personal appearance was as
notable. He was almost six feet in height, perfectly propor-
tioned, and in figure and deportment he was the most manly
man I have ever met. His chest was broad; his muscles
were firm; his face wore a most benign expression; his complexion was roseate; his eyes were light blue and beamed
with intelligence; his hair was soft and light brown in
color, and his speech was rather low, sweet, and musical,
His personal beauty and grace of manner were most charming. Why, all the girls in New Haven fell in love with
him," said Dr. Munson, "and wept tears of real sorrow
when they heard of his sad fate. In dress he was always
neat; he was quick to lend a helping hand to a being in dis-
tress, brute or human; was overflowing with good-humor,
and was the idol of all his acquaintances."

Such was the verbal testimony of a personal acquaintance of Nathan Hale as to his appearance and character

when he left Yale College.*   Dr. Jared Sparks, who knew
several of Hale's intimate friends, writes of him :

FAC-SIMILE OF HALE'S HAND-WRITING.

"Possessing genius, taste, and order, he became distinguished as a scholar; and, endowed in an eminent degree
with those graces and gifts of Nature which add a charm to
youthful excellence, he gained universal esteem and confidence.   To high moral worth and irreproachable habits
were joined gentleness of manner, an ingenuous disposition,

---

* Dr. Munson allowed me to read the following letter written by Hale to his
father, from New London, late in September, 1774, and to make a *fac-simile* of
the last paragraph as seen above :

"NEW LONDON, *November* 30, 1774.

"SIR : I am very happily situated here.   I love my employment ; find many
friends among strangers ; have time for scientific study, and seem to fill the place
assigned me with satisfaction.   I have a school of more than thirty boys to instruct,
about half of them in Latin ; and my salary is satisfactory.   During the summer I
had a morning class of young ladies—about a score—from five to seven o'clock ; so
you see my time is pretty fully occupied, profitably I hope to my pupils and to
their teacher.

"Please accept for yourself and Mrs. Munson the grateful thanks of one who
will always remember the kindness he ever experienced whenever he visited your
abode.   Your friend,   NATHAN HALE."

and vigor of understanding. No young man of his years put forth a fairer promise of future usefulness and celebrity; the fortunes of none were fostered more sincerely by the generous good wishes of his associates, and the hopes and encouraging presages of his superiors.

Among Hale's classmates was (afterward Major) Benjamin Tallmadge, who had charge of André soon after his arrest. With William Robinson and Ezra Samson he was engaged with Hale at their graduation, in a Latin syllogistic dispute, followed by a debate on the question, " Whether the education of daughters be not, without any just reason, more neglected than that of the sons?"

"In this debate Hale was triumphant," wrote James Hillhouse, another of his classmates, who was a few months his junior. "He was the champion of 'The Daughters,' and most ably advocated their cause. You may be sure that he received the plaudits of the ladies present."

On leaving college, Hale engaged in school-teaching for nearly two years. He first taught a select school at East Haddam, on the left bank of the Connecticut River, then a place of much wealth.

In 1774 he was called to the position of preceptor in the Union Grammar-School at New London, an institution of high grade, intended to furnish facilities for a thorough English education and the classical preparation necessary for entering college. The school-building stood on State Street. Young Hale was appointed its first preceptor after its organization. It was a high compliment to his ability.

Hale's connection with this school was most agreeable. Everybody became warmly attached to him. His life moved on in a placid current, with scarcely a ripple upon its surface. He assiduously cultivated science and letters, moved in the most refined society, and engaged in social pleasures and religious repose. His future appeared full of joyful promises.

UNION GRAMMAR SCHOOL-HOUSE AT NEW LONDON.

Suddenly war's alarms dispelled Hale's dream of quiet happiness. The news of the bloodshed at Lexington and Concord aroused the continent—New England in a special manner. A messenger, riding express with the news, between Boston and New York, brought it to New London late on the 21st of April. It created intense excitement. A town meeting was called at the court-house at twilight. Among the speakers present whose words fired the hearts of the eager listeners was Nathan Hale. With impassioned language and intense earnestness he exhorted the people to take patriotic action at once. "Let us march immediately," he cried, "and never lay down our arms until we have obtained our independence!" This was the first public demand for independence made at the beginning of the great struggle.

When the meeting adjourned, Hale, with others, enrolled himself as a volunteer. A company was soon formed. On the following morning when the school assembled, he prayed with his pupils, gave them good advice, bade each one of them an affectionate farewell, and soon afterward departed for Cambridge. He returned and resumed his duties at the school, but it was not long before his intense desire to serve his country caused him to enlist as a lieutenant of a company in Colonel Charles Webb's regiment—a body raised by order of the General Assembly for home defense, or, if necessary, for the protection of the country at large.

Late in September Hale marched with his régiment to Cambridge, and participated in the siege of Boston. He received the commission of captain early in January, and was vigilant and brave at all times. The British were driven from the New England capital in March (1776), and sailed away to Halifax with a host of Tories, who fled from the wrath of the Whigs whom they had oppressed. After the British left Boston, the bulk of the American army proceeded to New York. So earnest and unselfish was Hale's patriotism that, when, late in 1775, the men of his company, whose term of service had expired, determined to return home, he offered to give them his month's pay if they would remain so much longer.

Soon after Hale's arrival at New York, he successfully performed a daring feat. A British sloop, laden with provisions, was anchored in the East River under the protection of the guns of the man-of-war *Asia* sixty-four. General Heath gave Hale permission to attempt the capture of the supply-vessel. With a few picked men (probably of Glover's brigade, who were largely seamen), as resolute as himself, he proceeded in a whale-boat silently at midnight to the side of the sloop, unobserved by the sentinel on the deck. Hale and his men sprang on board, secured the sentinel, confined the crew below the hatches, raised her anchor, and took her into Coenties Slip just at the dawn of day. Captain Hale was at the helm. The victors were greeted, with loud huzzas from a score of voices when the sloop touched the wharf. The stores of provisions of the prize-vessel were distributed among Hale's hungry fellow-soldiers.

We have no information concerning Hale's movements from the time of his capture of the supply-vessel until after the battle of Long Island. He became captain of a company of Connecticut Rangers in May—a corps composed of choice men picked from the different Connecticut regiments, and placed under the command of Lieutenant-Colonel Thomas Knowlton, who had distinguished himself in the battle of Bunker's (Breed's) Hill. They were known as "Congress's Own."

In two or three letters written by Hale to his brothers in the earlier part of the summer, he mentions some hostile movements, but there are no indications that he was engaged in any of them. He seems not to have been in the battle of Long Island or a participant in the famous retreat of Washington across the East River, from Brooklyn, at the close of August. He was among the troops that remained in New York when the British invaded Long Island (for he was sick at that time), and joined the retreating forces in their march toward Harlem Heights early in September. He first appears after that movement in the presence of Washington, at the house of the opulent Quaker merchant, Robert Murray, on Murray Hill, to receive instructions for the performance of an important mission. What was the nature of that mission? Let us see:

The American army on Manhattan Island was in a most perilous condition after the retreat from Long Island. It was fearfully demoralized, and seemed to be on the point of dissolution. Despair had taken possession of the minds of the militia. They deserted by companies and even by regiments. Impatient of restraint, insubordination everywhere prevailed. The soldiers clamored for pay; the money-chest was empty. They clamored for clothing and blankets, as cold weather was approaching; the commissary could not respond. One third of the men were without tents, and one fourth of them were on the sick-roll. Only fourteen thousand men were fit for duty, and these were scattered in detachments lying between each extremity of the island, a distance of a dozen miles or more.

The British army was then twenty-five thousand strong, and lay in compact detachments along the shores of New York Bay and the East River, from (present) Greenwood Cemetery to Flushing and beyond. The soldiers were veterans, and were flushed with the recent victory. They were commanded by able generals. The army was supported by a powerful naval force which studded with armed vessels the waters that clasped Manhattan Island. Each arm of the service was magnificently equipped with artillery, stores, and munitions of war of every kind.

Such was the condition and relative position of the two armies when, on the 7th of September, Washington called a council of war to consider the important questions, What shall be done? Shall we defend or abandon New York?

Washington had already asked Congress, " If we should be obliged to abandon the town, ought it to stand as winter-

quarters for the enemy?" He was answered by a resolve
that, in case he should find it necessary that he should quit
New York, he should " have special care taken that no dam-
age be done to the city, Congress having no doubt of their
being able to recover it." It was resolved to remain and
defend the city.

CHAPTER II.

PERILS were· gathering thick and fast, and at another
council, held on the 12th, it was resolved to abandon the
city and take a position on Harlem Heights. The sick were
sent over to New Jersey, and the public stores were taken'
to Dobb's Ferry, twenty miles up the Hudson River. Then
the main army moved northward, leaving in the city a
guard of four thousand men under General Putnam, with
orders to follow if necessary.

Washington made his headquarters at the house of Robert Murray on the 14th. The position of the American
army now appeared more perilous than ever. Two ships-
of-war had passed up the East River. Others soon followed.
Scouts reported active movements among the British troops
everywhere, but could not penetrate, even by reasonable
conjecture, the designs of the enemy. It was of the utmost
importance to know something of their real intentions.
Washington wrote to General Heath, then stationed at
Kingsbridge:

"As everything, in a manner, depends upon obtaining intelligence of the enemy's motions, I do most earnestly entreat you and General Clinton to exert yourselves to accom-
plish this most desirable end. Leave no stone unturned, nor

do not stick at expense, to bring this to pass, as I was never more uneasy than on account of my want of knowledge on this score. Keep constant lookout, with good glasses, on some commanding heights that look well on to the other shore."

The vital questions pressing for answer were, Will they make a direct attack upon the city? Will they land upon the island, above the city, or at Morrisania beyond the Harlem River? Will they attempt to cut off our communications with the main, by seizing the region along the Harlem River or at Kingsbridge, by landing forces on the shores of the East and Hudson Rivers, at Turtle Bay, or at Bloomingdale, and, stretching a cordon of armed men from river to river, cut off the four thousand troops left in the city?

Washington, in his perplexity, called another council of war at Murray's. He told his officers that he could not procure the least information concerning the intentions of the enemy, and asked the usual question of late, What shall be done? It was resolved to send a competent person, in disguise, into the British camps on Long Island to unveil the momentous secret. It needed one skilled in military and scientific knowledge and a good draughtsman; a man possessed of a quick eye, a cool head, unflinching courage; tact, caution, and sagacity—a man on whose judgment and fidelity implicit reliance might be placed.

Washington sent for Lieutenant-Colonel Knowlton and asked him to seek for a trustful man for the service, in his own noted regiment or in some other. Knowlton summoned a large number of officers to a conference at his quarters, and, in the name of the commander-in-chief, invited a volunteer for the important service. They were surprised. There was a long pause. Patriotism, ambition, a love of adventure, and indignation, alternately took possession of their feelings. It was an invitation to serve their country supremely by becoming a spy—a character upon whom all civilized nations place the ban of scorn and contumely! They recoiled from such a service, and there was a general and even resentful refusal to comply with the request.

Late in the conference, when Knowlton had despaired of finding a man competent and willing to undertake the perilous mission, a young officer appeared, pale from the effects of recent severe sickness. Knowlton repeated the invitation, when, almost immediately, the voice of the young soldier was heard uttering the momentous words, " I will undertake it!" It was the voice of Captain Nathan Hale.

Everybody was astonished. The whole company knew Hale. They loved and admired him. They tried to dissuade him from his decision, setting forth the risk of sacrificing all his good prospects in life and the fond hopes of his parents and friends. They painted in darkest colors the ignominy and death to which he might be exposed. His warmly attached friend, William Hull (afterward a general in the War of 1812), who was a member of his company and had been a classmate at college, employed all the force of friendship and the arts of persuasion to bend him from his purpose, but in vain. With warmth and decision Hale said : - ·

"Gentlemen, I think I owe to my country the accomplishment of an object so important and so much desired by the commander of her armies, and I know no mode of obtaining the information but by assuming a disguise and passing into the enemy's camp. I am fully sensible of the consequences of discovery and capture in such a situation. But for a year I have been attached to the army, and have

not rendered any material service, while receiving a com-
pensation for which I make no return. Yet I am not influ-
enced by any expectation of promotion or pecuniary reward.
I wish to be useful; *and every kind of service necessary for the
public good becomes honorable by being necessary.* If the exigencies of my country demand a peculiar service, its claims to
the performance of that service are imperious.",

These manly, wise, and patriotic words—this willingness
to sacrifice himself, if necessary, for the good of his country
—silenced his brother officers. Accompanied by Knowlton,
he appeared before Washington the same afternoon, and
received instructions concerning his mission. His commander also furnished him with a general order to the
owners of all American vessels in Long Island Sound to
convey him to any point on Long Island which he might
designate.

Hale left the camp on Harlem Heights the same evening,
accompanied by Sergeant Stephen Hempstead, a trustworthy member of his company, whom he engaged to go
with him as far as it would be prudent. He was also accompanied by his trusty servant, Ansel Wright. They found
no safe place to cross the Sound until they arrived at Norwalk, fifty miles from New York, owing to the presence of
small British cruisers in those waters. There Hale exchanged his regimentals for a citizen's dress of brown cloth
and a broad-brimmed round hat, and directed Hempstead
and Wright to tarry for him at Norwalk until his return,
which he supposed would be on the 20th. He directed a
boat to be sent for him on the morning of that day, and left
with Hempstead his uniform and his military commission
and other papers.

There are somewhat conflicting accounts concerning

Hale's movements after he left Norwalk. All agree that he was conveyed across the Sound to Huntington Bay, where he landed; that he assumed the character of a schoolmaster and loyalist disgusted with the "rebel" cause, and that he professed to be in quest of an engagement as a school-teacher. It is known that he entered the British camps in personal disguise and with the pretext of loyalty and the character of a pedagogue; that he was received with great cordiality as a "good fellow"; that he visited all the British camps on Long Island, made observations openly, and draw-ings and memoranda of fortifications, etc., secretly; that he passed over from Brooklyn to New York city and gathered much information concerning affairs there, the British hav-ing invaded Manhattan Island and secured possession of the town since his departure;* and that he returned to Long Island and passed through the various camps to Huntington Bay for the purpose of going back to Norwalk.

Tradition tells us that Hale was conveyed from Norwalk to Huntington Bay on a sloop, and was landed from her yawl two hours before daybreak in the neighborhood of a place called "The Cedars." Near there a Widow Chiches-ter, a stanch loyalist (called "Widow Chich"), kept a tav-ern, which was the resort of all the Tories in that region. Hale passed this dangerous place with safety before cock-crowing, and at a farm-house a mile distant he was kindly furnished with breakfast and a bed for repose after his night's toil. Then he made his way to the nearest British

---

* On the day after Hale's departure, a strong British force crossed the East River and landed at Kip's Bay at the foot of (present) Thirty-fourth Street, drove off an American detachment stationed there, and formed a line almost across the isl-and to Bloomingdale. On the 16th detachments of the two armies had a severe con-test on Harlem Plains, in which the Americans were victorious, but at the cost of the life of the gallant Colonel Knowlton.

camp, and was received without suspicion of his real character. Concerning his movements after that, until his return from New York, tradition is silent.

Hale, on his return, had reached in safety the point on the Long Island shore where he first landed, and prepared to recross the sound at Norwalk the next morning. He wore shoes with loose inner soles. Between the soles he had concealed the accurate drawings he had made of fortifications, etc., and also his memoranda, written in Latin on thin paper. He had given directions for the boat, from which he had landed, to come for him on a designated morning, which would be the next after his return. Satisfied that he was safe from harm, for he was remote from a British post, and happy with the thought that his perilous mission was ended successfully and that he should render his country most important service, he awaited the coming morning with patience and serenity of mind.

Feeling secure in his simple dress and disguised manner, Hale entered the tavern of the Widow Chichester, at " The Cedars." A number of persons were in the room. A moment afterward, a man, whose face seemed familiar to him, suddenly departed and was not seen again.

Hale passed the night at the tavern, and at dawn went out to look for the expected boat. To his great joy he saw one moving toward the shore, with several men in it. Not doubting they were his friends, he hastened toward the beach, where, as the vessel touched the shore, he was astounded by the sight of a barge bearing British marines. He turned to flee, when a loud voice called, " Surrender or die!" Looking back he saw six men standing erect, with muskets leveled at him. He was seized, taken into the barge, and conveyed to the British guard-ship *Halifax*,

Captain Quarng, which was anchored behind a point of wooded land of Lloyd's Neck.

It has been asserted that the man who so suddenly departed from the room of the tavern at "The Cedars" when Hale entered was a Tory cousin of his, a dissipated fellow, who recognized his kinsman in disguise and betrayed him into the hands of the enemy; but there is no warrant for such an accusation.

Hale's captors stripped and searched him, and found the evidences of his being a spy in the papers concealed between the soles of his shoes. These formed as positive tes-

THE BEEKMAN MANSION.

timony as to his true character as did the papers found in André's boot, which convicted the adjutant-general of the British army of being a spy.

Captain Hale was taken in one of the boats of the *Hali-*

fax to General Howe's headquarters, at the elegant mansion of James Beekman, at Mount Pleasant, as the high bank of the East River at Turtle Bay was called. The house was situated at (present) Fifty-first Street and First Avenue. It was then deserted by its stanch Whig owner. Around it

BEEKMAN'S GREENHOUSE.

were beautiful lawns and blooming gardens; and near it was a greenhouse filled with exotic shrubbery and plants.* In that greenhouse Hale was confined, under a strong guard, on Saturday night, the 21st of September. He had

---

* I made a sketch of the Beekman mansion in 1849, and of the greenhouse in 1852, a few days before it was demolished, with all the glories of the garden, at Mount Pleasant; for, at the behest of the Street Commissioner, streets were opened through the whole Beekman domain. The site of the greenhouse was in the center of (present) Fifty-second Street, a little east of First Avenue. It was erected with the mansion in 1764. The mansion was occupied, during the war, as headquarters by Generals Howe, Clinton, and Robertson. It was the residence of the Brunswick General Riedesel and his family in the summer of 1780. General Carleton occupied it in 1783.

3

been taken before Howe, who, without trial, and upon the
evidence found in his shoes, condemned him to be hanged
early the next morning. Howe delivered him into the custody of William Cunningham, the notorious British provost-
marshal, with orders to execute him before sunrise the next
day.

This severity, nay, absolute inhumanity, was doubtless
the result of great irritation of the minds of the British officers at that moment. They had looked upon the little city
of New York, containing twenty thousand inhabitants, as a
most comfortable place for their winter-quarters. On the
very morning when Hale was arrested (at a little past midnight), a fearful conflagration was accidentally begun at a low
tavern on the wharf near Whitehåll Slip (now Staten Island
Ferry). Swiftly the flames spread, and were not quenched
until about five hundred buildings were consumed. The
British believed, and so declared, that the fire was the work
of Whig incendiaries, to deprive the army of comforts. The
city was yet ablaze while Hale was lying in Beekman's
greenhouse, awaiting his doom in the early morning.

When Hale was taken before Howe, he frankly acknowl-
edged his rank and his purpose as a spy. He firmly but re-
spectfully told of his success in getting information in the
British camps, and, expressed his regret that he had not
been able to serve his country better. "I was present at
this interview," wrote a British officer, "and I observed that
the frankness, the manly bearing, and the evident disinterested patriotism of the handsome young prisoner, sensibly
touched a tender chord of General Howe's nature ; but the
stern rules of war concerning such offenses would not allow
him to exercise even pity."

CHAPTER III.

LONG before daybreak of a Christian Sabbath, Nathan Hale was marched to the place of execution, in the vicinity of (present) [East Broadway and Market Street.] He was escorted by a file of soldiers, and there delivered to the pro-vóst-marshal. The young commander of a British detach-ment lying near, told Captain William Hull that on Hale's arrival he requested Cunningham to allow him to sit in his (the officer's) marquee while waiting for the necessary prepa-rations. The boon was granted. [Hale requested the pres-ence of a chaplain; it was denied.] He asked for a Bible; it was refused. At the solicitation of the compassionate young officer in whose tent Hale sat, he was allowed to write brief letters to his mother, sisters, and the young maiden to whom he was betrothed; * but, when they were handed to the pro-vost-marshal to cause them to be forwarded, that officer read them. He grew furious as he perceived the noble spirit which breathed in every sentence, and with coarse oaths and foul epithets he tore them into shreds before the face of his young victim. Hale gave Cunningham a withering glance of scorn, and then resumed his usual calmness and

---

* Her name was Alice Adams. She was a native of Canterbury, Connecticut, and was distinguished both for her intelligence and personal beauty. After Hale's death she married Eleazar Ripley, who left her a widow, with one child, at the age of eighteen years. The child died about a year after its father's death, and the mother subsequently married William Lawrence, of Hartford, where she lived until September, 1845, when she died at the age of eighty-eight years. She possessed a miniature of Hale and many of his letters. The miniature and the letters disap-peared many years ago, and there is no likeness of the young martyr extant. The last words uttered by Hale's betrothed were, " Write to Nathan ! "—Stuart's " Life of Nathan Hale," p. 28.

dignity of demeanor. The provost-marshal afterward said
that he destroyed the epistles "that the rebels should never
know that they had a man who could die with such firmness."

CUNNINGHAM DESTROYING HALE'S LETTERS.

It was in the morning twilight of a beautiful September
day that Hale was led out to execution. The gallows was

the limb of an apple-tree in Colonel Rutgers's orchard.* Even at that early hour quite a large number of men and women had gathered to witness the sad scene. Cunningham watched every arrangement with evident satisfaction; and, when everything was ready for the last scene in the tragedy, he scoffingly demanded of his victim his "last dying speech and confession!"

The soul of the young martyr, patriot, and hero, who was standing upon the fatal ladder † with his eyes turned heavenward, was then in secret communion with his Maker, and his mortal ears seemed closed to earthly sounds. He did not notice the insulting words of the human fiend. A moment afterward he looked benignly upon the evidently sympathetic spectators, and with a calm, clear voice pronounced the last words uttered by him:

"I only regret that I have but one life to lose for my country!"

---

* The place of Hale's execution has been a subject of conjecture. Some have supposed that it occurred near the Beekman mansion, Howe's headquarters ; others, that he was taken from the Provost Prison (now the Hall of Records), in the City Hall Park, to the usual place of execution of state criminals, at the Barracks near Chambers Street ; and others, on the farm of Colonel Rutgers, whose country mansion was near the East River—at Pike and Monroe Streets.

In 1849 I visited the venerable Jeremiah Johnson, ex-Mayor of Brooklyn, who was living at his farm-house not far from the Navy-Yard, then between the city of Brooklyn and the village of Williamsburgh. Among other interesting facts concerning the Revolution, of his own experience and observation, which he had treasured in his memory, was that his father was present at the execution of Hale. Like other Long Island farmers at that time, he went to New York occasionally with truck. On the day of the great fire he was there, when himself and his team were pressed into the service of the British. He was with the detachment on Colonel Rutgers's farm at the time of the execution, and saw the martyr hanged upon the limb of an apple-tree in Rutgers's orchard. It was at the west side, not far from the line of (present) East Broadway.

† The method employed at military executions at that time was to place a ladder against the gallows-beam or limb, cause the prisoner to ascend it a few feet, and, at a given signal, turn the ladder and leave the victim suspended.

The women wept; some of them sobbed audibly. The sublime and burning words of the victim about to be sacrificed upon the altar of liberty, and the visible tokens of sympathy among those who witnessed the scene, maddened the coarse-natured and malignant provost-marshal.* He cried out in a voice hoarse with anger, "Swing the rebel off!" and cursed the tearful women with foul imprecations, calling them rebels and harlots!

So ended, in an atmosphere of mingled Christian faith, fortitude, and hope, and of savage barbarism and brutality, the beautiful life-drama of Nathan Hale, the early martyr for the cause of human freedom in the grand struggle for the independence of our country. It is a cause for just reproach of our people that their history, poetry, oratory, and art have, for more than a century, neglected to erect a fitting memorial to his memory—either in the literature of the land he so loved that he freely gave his young life a sacrifice for its salvation from bondage, or in bronze or marble. Nowhere in our broad domain, stretching from sea to sea, teeming with almost sixty million freemen, is there even a mural tablet seen with the name of Nathan Hale upon it, excepting a small monument in his native town, overlooking

---

* The pen of every writer who has noticed the career of William Cunningham, the notorious provost-marshal of the British army in New York and Philadelphia, has portrayed him as a most detestable character. To the credit of the commander with whom he served, be it said that it is satisfactorily proven that he was employed directly by the British ministry, and was independent of the authority of Howe and Clinton. He was a large, burly, red-haired, red-faced Irishman, sixty years of age, addicted to strong drink to excess, and with most forbidding features. His cruelties and crimes committed while in charge of prisoners of war in New York were notorious and monstrous. Upon the scaffold in England, after the war, he confessed that he had caused the death of fully two thousand prisoners under his charge by starvation and otherwise. He put poison into their food at times, and sold their rations for his own benefit, allowing the prisoners to starve!

the graves of his kindred, in an obscure church-yard, which was erected forty years ago.)

The body of the martyr was laid in the earth near the spot where his spirit left it. A British officer was sent to acquaint Washington with his fate. A rude stone placed by the side of the grave of his father, in the burial-ground of the Congregational Church in his native town, for long years revealed to passers-by the fact that it was in commemoration of "Nathan Hale, Esq., a captain in the army of the United States, who was born June 6, 1755, received the first honors of Yale College, September, 1773," and "resigned his life a sacrifice to his country's liberty at New York, September 22, 1776, aged twenty-two." An entry of his death was made upon the town records of Coventry.

Late in November, 1837—sixty-one years after his sacrifice—the citizens of Coventry formed a "Hale Monument Association" for the purpose of raising funds for the erection of a suitable memorial to the memory of the young patriot. The association applied in vain to Congress for aid. By fairs, tea-parties, private dramatic performances, and other social appliances, carried on chiefly by the gentler sex, and a grant of twelve hundred dollars by the State of Connecticut, a sufficient sum was secured in 1846 to erect the desired monument.

At one of the fairs, a poem, addressed to "The Daughters of Freedom," and printed on white satin, was offered for sale, and was widely distributed. It contained the following verses:

"Ye come with hearts that oft have glowed
  At his soul-stirring tale,
To wreath the deathless evergreen
  Around the name of Hale.

THE HALE MONUMENT AT COVENTRY.

" Here his memorial stone shall rise
In freedom's hallowed shade,
Prouder than André's trophied tomb
'Mid mightiest monarchs laid."

The Hale memorial stands upon elevated ground near
the Congregational Church in South Coventry, and by the
side of the old burial-ground in which repose the remains of
his nearest kindred. Toward the north it overlooks the
beautiful Lake Waugumbaug, in the pellucid waters of which
Hale angled in his boyhood and early youth.

The monument was designed by Henry Austin, of New
Haven, and was erected under the superintendence of Solo-
mon Willard, the architect of the Bunker's Hill Monument.
It was completed in the summer of 1846, at a cost of three
thousand seven hundred and thirty-four dollars. The material is Quincy granite. Its form is seen in the engraving.
The height is forty-five feet, and it is fourteen feet square at
its base. The pedestal bears on its four sides the following
inscriptions:

North side: " CAPTAIN NATHAN HALE, 1776." *West
side:* " Born at Coventry, June 6, 1755." *East side:* " Died
at New York, September 22, 1776." *South side:* " I REGRET
THAT I HAVE BUT ONE LIFE TO LOSE FOR MY COUNTRY."

The fate of young Hale produced universal sorrow in
the Continental army and among the patriotic people. In
the Whig newspapers of the day tributes to his worth as a
man and a patriot appeared in both prose and verse.* Dur-

---

* A ballad was written and published, soon after Hale's death, which was very
popular at the time. It was evidently written by one who was not well informed
as to the true history of the matter. Of his arrest the ballad says:

" Cooling shades of the night were coming apace,
The tattoo had beat, the tattoo had beat,
The noble one sprang from his dark lurking-place,
To make his retreat, to make his retreat.

ing the War of 1812'–15, a little fort, erected upon Black
Rock, at the entrance to New Haven Harbor, on the site of
a smaller one, built during the Revolution, was named Fort
Hale, the first monument of stone that commemorated him.
It has long been in ruins. Then followed the simple structure built by his neighbors at Coventry. Brief notices of
the martyr have been given from time to time in occasional
poetic effusions and/in oratory. Timothy Dwight, Hale's
tutor at Yale-College, and afterward president of that institution, wrote:

> " Thus while fond Virtue wished in vain to save,
> HALE, bright and generous, found a hapless grave;
> With genius' living flame his bosom glowed,
> And Science lured him to her sweet abode.
> In Worth's fair path his feet adventured far,
> The pride of peace, the rising hope of war;
> In duty firm, in danger calm as even,
> To friends unchanging, and sincere to Heaven.
> How short his course, the prize how early won!
> While weeping Friendship mourns her favorite gone."

I. W. Stuart, in his little biography of Hale,* has preserved fragments of several poetic effusions. A short time
after Hale's death, an unknown personal friend of the martyr wrote a poem of one hundred and sixty lines, in which
he described the personal appearance of the young soldier—

> " He warily trod on the dry, rustling leaves
>   As he passed through the wood, as he passed through the wood,
> And silently gained his rude launch on the shore,
>   As she played with the flood, as she played with the flood.

> " The guards of the camp on that dark, dreary night
>   Had a murderous will, a murderous will;
> They took him and bore him afar from the shore,
>   To a hut on the hill, to a hut on the hill."

* " Life of Captain Nathan Hale, the Martyr Spy of the American Revolution."
By I. W. Stuart, Hartford, 1856.

tall and with "a beauteous face." Of his qualities of temper
and conduct he wrote:

> " Removed from envy, malice, pride, and strife,
> He walked through goodness as he walked through life;
> A kinder brother Nature never knew,
> A child more duteous or a friend more true."

Of Hale's motives in becoming a spy he wrote:

> " Hate of oppression's arbitrary plan,
> The love of freedom, and the rights of man;
> A strong desire to save from slavery's chain
> The future millions of the Western main."

The poet follows him in his career until he enters upon
his perilous mission under instructions from Washington.
Of the final scene he wrote:

> " Not Socrates or noble Russell died,
> Or gentle Sidney, Britain's boast and pride,
> Or gen'rous Moore, approached life's final goal,
> With more composed, more firm and stable soul."

J. S. Babcock, of Coventry, wrote in the metre of Wolfe's
" Sir John Moore ":

> " He fell in the spring of his early prime,
> With his fair hopes all around him ;
> He died for his birth-land—a 'glorious crime '—
> Ere the palm of his fame had crowned him.

> " He fell in her darkness—he lived not to see
> The noon of her risen glory ;
> But the name of the brave, in the hearts of the free,
> Shall be twined in her deathless glory."

In a poem delivered before the Linonian Society of Yale
College, at its centennial anniversary in 1853, a society of
which Hale was a member, Francis M. Finch said, in allusion to the martyr:

" To drum-beat and heart-beat,
    A soldier marches by ;
There is color on his cheek,
    There is courage in his eye ;
Yet to drum-beat and heart-beat
    In a moment he must die.

" By starlight and moonlight
    He seeks the Briton's camp ;
He hears the rustling flag,
    And that armèd sentry's tramp ;
And the starlight and moonlight
    His silent wanderings lamp.

" With slow tread, and still tread,
    He scans thè tented line ;
And he counts the battery-guns
    By the gaunt and shadowy pine ;
And his slow tread and still tread
    Gives no warning sign.

" The dark wave, the plumed wave,
    It meets his eager glance,
And it sparkles 'neath the stars
    Like the glimmer of a lance ;
A dark wave, a plumed wave,
    On an emerald expanse.

    .   .   .   .

" With calm brow, steady brow,
    He listens to his doom ;
In his look there is no fear,
    Nor a shadow trace of gloom ;
And with calm brow and steady brow
    He robes him for the tomb.

" In the long night, the still night,
    He kneels upon the sod ;
And the brutal guards withhold
    E'en the solemn Word of God !
In the long night, the still night,
    He walks where Christ hath trod !

" 'Neath the blue morn, the sunny morn,
  He dies upon the tree ;
And he mourns that he can lose
  But one life for Liberty ;
And in the blue morn, the sunny morn
  His spirit-wings are free !

.   .   .   .

" From fame-leaf and angel-leaf,
  From monument and urn,
The sad of earth, the glad of heaven,
  His tragic fate shall learn ;
And on fame-leaf and angel-leaf
  The name of HALE shall burn ! "

At the dedication of a monument in 1853, erected on the
spot near Tarrytown where André was captured, the late
Henry J. Raymond, in an address on the occasion, said :

"At an early stage of the Revolution, NATHAN HALE,
captain in the American army, which he had entered, aban-
doning brilliant prospects of professional distinction for the
sole purpose of defending the liberties of his country—gifted,
educated, ambitious—the equal of André in talent, in worth,
in amiable manners, and in every manly quality, and his superior in that final test of character—the motives by which
his acts were prompted and his life was guided—laid aside
every consideration personal to himself, and entered upon a
service of infinite hazard to life and honor, because Washington deemed it important to the sacred cause to which
both had been sacredly set apart. Like André, he was
found in the hostile camp ; like him, though without trial,
he was adjudged as a spy ; and, like him, he was condemned to death.

" And here the likeness ends. No consoling word, no
pitying or respectful look, cheered the dark hours of his
doom. He was met with insult at every turn. The sacred

consolations of the minister of God were denied him ; the Bible was taken from him ; with an excess of barbarity hard to be paralleled in civilized war, his dying letters of farewell to his mother and sisters were destroyed in his presence ; and, uncheered by sympathy, mocked by brutal power, and attended only by that sense of duty, incorruptible, undefiled, which had ruled his life—finding a fit farewell in the serene and sublime regret that he had 'but *one* life to lose for his country '—he went forth to meet the great darkness of an ignominious death.

" The loving hearts of his early companions have erected a neat monument to his memory in his native town ; but, beyond that little circle, where stands his name recorded ? While the majesty of England, in the person of her sovereign, sent an embassy across the sea to solicit the remains of André at the hands of his foes, that they might be enshrined in that sepulchre where she garners the relics of her mighty and renowned sons—

' Splendid in their ashes, pompous in the grave,'

the children of Washington have left the body of HALE to sleep in its unknown tomb, though it be on his native soil, unhonored by any outward observance, unmarked by any memorial stone. Monody, eulogy, monument of marble or of brass, and of letters more enduring than all, have in his own land and in ours given the name and fate of André to the sorrowing remembrance of all time to come. American genius has celebrated his praises, has sung of his virtues, and exalted to heroic heights his prayer, manly but personal to himself, for choice in the manner of death—his dying challenge to all men to witness the courage with which he met his fate. But where, save on the cold page of history,

stands the record of HALE? Where is the hymn that speaks
to immortality, and tells of the added brightness and en-
hanced glory when his soul joined its noble host? And
where sleep the American of Americans, that their hearts
are not stirred to solemn rapture at the thought of the sublime love of country which buoyed him not alone 'above the
fear of death,' but far beyond all thought of himself, of his
fate and his fame, or of anything less than his country—and
which shaped his dying breath into the sacred sentence
which trembled at the last upon his quivering lip ?"

. These eloquent words have a deeper significance to-day
than when they were uttered a generation ago. It is a just
reproach to a nation of nearly sixty million freemen, rich
and powerful beyond any other people on the globe, that the
memory of NATHAN HALE, their self-sacrificing benefactor
in purpose, and a true and noble martyr in the cause of the
liberty they enjoy, has been, until lately, absolutely neglected
by them ; that no " monody, eulogy, monument of marble or
of brass," dedicated to him by the public voice, appears any-
where in our broad land. But there are now abundant
promises that this reproach will be speedily removed. An
earnest effort was begun by the " Daily Telegraph," a morning journal of New York city, late in 1885, to procure funds
by half-dime or "nickel" subscriptions, sufficient to erect a
suitable monument to the memory of NATHAN HALE, in the
city of New York, where he suffered martyrdom. There is
also a project on foot for the erection of a statue of Hale in
the Connecticut State Capitol at Hartford. For this purpose the State of Connecticut has appropriated five thousand dollars.

Let the conscience of our people, inspired by gratitude
and patriotism, be fairly awakened to the propriety of the

undertaking, and funds will speedily be forthcoming sufficient to erect a magnificent monument in memory of
NATHAN HALE, in the city where he died for his country.
I recommend, as a portion of the inscription upon the monument, the subjoined epitaph, written fully thirty years ago,
by George Gibbs, the ripe scholar and antiquary, who was at
one time the librarian of the New York Historical Society: *

" STRANGER, BENEATH THIS STONE
LIES THE DUST OF
A SPY,
WHO PERISHED UPON THE GIBBET ;
YET
THE STORIED MARBLES OF THE GREAT,
THE SHRINES OF HEROES,
ENTOMBED NOT ONE MORE WORTHY OF
HONOR
THAN HIM WHO HERE
SLEEPS HIS LAST SLEEP.
NATIONS ·
BOW WITH REVERENCE BEFORE THE DUST
OF HIM WHO DIES
A GLORIOUS DEATH,
URGED ON BY THE SOUND OF THE
TRUMPET
AND THE SHOUTS OF
ADMIRING THOUSANDS.
BUT WHAT REVERENCE, WHAT HONOR,
IS NOT DUE TO ONE
WHO FOR HIS COUNTRY ENCOUNTERED
EVEN AN INFAMOUS DEATH,
SOOTHED BY NO SYMPATHY,
ANIMATED BY NO PRAISE !

---

* A statue in plaster, modeled from a description of Hale's features and person,
has been made by E. S. Wood, sculptor. It represents an athletic young man, with
his coat and vest removed, his neck and upper portion of his chest bared by the
turning down of the collar of his ruffled shirt, and holding in his right hand, which
is resting upon his hip, the rope with which he is about to be suspended from the
tree. The face of the martyr is an excellent ideal of the character of the young
hero.

JOHN ANDRÉ.

4

John André

JOHN ANDRÉ.

CHAPTER I.

IT is not known whether the place of JOHN ANDRÉ'S nativity was in London or elsewhere in England. His father was a Switzer, born in Geneva. He was a merchant in London, where he married a pretty French maiden named Girardot, a native of that city, who in the year 1751 became the mother of the famous British spy.

Of André's childhood and early youth very little is known, even of the scenes of his primary education. Later, we find him at the University in Geneva ; and, when he was approaching young manhood, he was distinguished for many accomplishments and solid acquirements. He had mastered several European languages, and was an expert mathematician. He was versed in military science, and had a wide acquaintance with *belles-lettres* literature. He was an adept in music, dancing, and the arts of design, and was specially commended for his military drawings.

André had a taste and a desire for military life ; but, before he was seventeen years of age, he was called home to take a place in his father's counting-room. At that time his family lived at the Manor House, Clapton, where his father died in the spring of 1769. The family then consisted of the widow, two sons, and three daughters. Of these John was the oldest and Anna was the youngest—the " tuneful

Anna," as Miss Seward calls her in her " Monody," because of her poetic genius.

John, though so young, was now a chief manager of his father's business and the head of his mother's household. The summer of 1769 was spent by the family at little villages in the interior of England, in the picturesque region of Lichfield, a famous cathedral town, in which Dr. Johnson was born, and at its grammar-school he and Addison and Garrick received their earlier education.

In that delightful neighborhood young André formed an acquaintance with Miss Anna Seward, the bright and charming daughter of Rev. Thomas Seward, canon-resident of Lichfield Cathedral, who lived in the bishop's palace. His daughter, then twenty-two years of age, was already distinguished as a poet. Her home was the gathering-place of the local literary celebrities of that day—Dr. Erasmus Darwin, author of " The Botanic Garden," and grandfather of the champion of the doctrine of evolution in our day; Thomas Hayley, author of " The Triumphs of Temper"; Sir Brooke Boothby, who wrote " Fables and Satires"; Richard Lovell Edgeworth, a "gay Lothario," with some literary pretensions; Thomas Day, an eccentric philosopher, who wrote the story of " Sandford and Merton," once as popular as " Robinson Crusoe"; the blind and ill-humored Miss Anna Williams, the biographer of the Emperor Julian; and other residents or occasional sojourners.

Miss Seward was the central figure in this literary circle. Her personal beauty, vivacity, wit, and charming conversational powers, were very fascinating. Into that galaxy John André was introduced and gave it additional luster.

The young London merchant also became acquainted with another maiden near his own age. She is represented as exceedingly lovely in person and character. Her eyes were blue, her hair was of a golden color, and her complexion was brilliant, heightened in its charms, perhaps, by a hectic glow upon her cheek—the sad prophecy of the early

HONORA SNEYD.—(From a painting by Romney.) *

fading of youthful beauty and of life. The maiden was Honora Sneyd, an inmate of the family of Canon Seward, and the loved companion of Anna.

André was then eighteen years of age ; a handsome, slender, graceful, and vivacious youth, with features as deli-

* In a letter to the Right Honorable Lady Butler, dated Lichfield, June 4, 1798, Miss Seward speaks of the picture as follows : " Honora Sneyd, after she became

cate as those of a girl, and accomplished beyond most young
men of his time. He was five feet nine inches in height,
dark complexion, dark eyes, brown hair, with a somewhat
serious and tender expression. His manners were easy and
insinuating. The young couple fell desperately in love with
each other at their first meeting.

Anna was delighted, and she fostered the passion. The
lovers were betrothed before the summer was over ; but
" Love's young dream " was disturbed. The father of Miss
Sneyd and the mother of André decided that both were too
young for wedlock then, and it was agreed that at least two
years should intervene between betrothal and nuptials. It
was also deemed proper that they should be kept apart as
much as possible during that period, in order to test the
strength and reality of their attachment, and for other pru-
dential reasons.

With this understanding André returned to his desk
in London, a hundred and twenty miles away. He had
sketched two miniatures of Miss Sneyd. One he gave to
Anna Seward, the other he placed in a locket and carried
it in his bosom. He also arranged for a correspondence
between Miss Seward and himself, of which Honora was to
be the chief burden. Three of these letters have been preserved, and are printed in this volume. " His epistolary
writings," says Dr. Sparks, " so far as specimens of them
have been preserved, show a delicacy of sentiment, a play-

Mrs. Edgeworth, sat to Smart, at that time a celebrated miniature-painter. He
totally missed the likeness which Major André had, from his then inexperience in
the art, so faintly and with so little justice to her beauty, caught. Romney accidentally, and without ever having beheld her, produced it completely. Yes, he
drew, to represent the Serena of the ' Triumph of Temper,' his own abstract idea
of perfect loveliness, and the form of the face of Honora Sneyd rose beneath his
pencil." Serena is represented reading by candle-light.

fulness of imagination, and an ease of style, which could proceed only from native refinement and a high degree of culture."

André had an aversion to mercantile pursuits, and had told his Lichfield friends that he greatly preferred the military profession. Miss Seward urged him to stick to his desk, as-the only sure promise of a competence which would enable him to marry Honora. Her persuasion prevailed, and he resolved to remain a merchant, for a time at least. In one of his letters to her he wrote :

" I know you will interest yourself in my destiny. I have now completely subdued my aversion to the profession of a merchant, and hope, in time, to acquire an inclination for it. . . . When an impertinent consciousness whispers in my ear that I am not of the right stuff for a merchant, I draw my Honora's picture from my bosom, and the sight of that dear talisman so inspires my industry that no toil seems oppressive."

This correspondence was kept up several months, but André's suit did not prosper. Distance, separation, and various circumstances cooled the ardor of Miss Sneyd's love for her young admirer, and correspondence between them ceased. She had other suitors ; and, in 1773, she married Richard Lovell Edgeworth, a gay young widower of twenty-five, who possessed a handsome fortune in the form of a fine estate in Ireland. Honora became the mother of Maria Edgeworth, the novelist. She died of consumption a few years afterward. In compliance with her dying request, her husband married her sister Elizabeth for his third wife.

André remained faithful to his first love, and carried Honora's miniature in his bosom until he died. He abandoned the mercantile business in 1771, joined the royal army with the commission of lieutenant in 1772, and went over to Germany. He joined his regiment — the Royal English Fusileers—in Canada, late in 1774, having made a farewell visit to his stanch friend Miss Seward before he sailed for America. During that visit a singular circumstance occurred. Miss Seward took André a little distance from Lichfield to call upon two literary friends, Mr. Cunningham, and a curate, the Rev. Mr. Newton. She had apprised them of the intended visit.

Mr. Cunningham afterward related to Miss Seward a singular dream he had on the night before this visit. He was in a great forest. A horseman approached at full speed. As he drew near, three men suddenly sprang from their concealment in bushes, seized the rider, and took him away. The appearance of the captive's face was deeply impressed upon the dreamer's memory. He awoke, fell asleep again, and dreamed. He was now in a vast crowd of people, near a great city. The man whom he saw captured in the forest was now brought forth and hanged. This dream was related to the curate the next morning, and when, a while afterward, Miss Seward with her friend arrived, Mr. Cunningham recognized in André the person he saw captured and hanged.

Other presaging visions concerning André's fate have been related, some of them being undoubtedly pure fiction. For example: Soon after the evacuation of Philadelphia by the British in 1778, and the Americans had taken possession of the city, some of the Continental officers gave a dinner-party to Washington at a spacious mansion in the suburbs, once belonging to one of the Penn family. At that banquet were two ladies who had known Major André during the British occupation, and had dined with him at this

Penn mansion. As they were passing through a grove near the house on that occasion, they both saw at the same moment the body of a man suspended from a limb, and recognized his features as those of André. They spoke of the vision at the table, and were laughed at; even Washington joining in the merriment. This ghost-story may be thus disposed of: Washington was not in Philadelphia at any time in the year 1778. At the time above mentioned he was chasing Sir Henry Clinton across New Jersey.

The following account appears to be well authenticated : A feminine friend of Miss Mary Hannah, a sister of André, shared a bed with her one night at about the time of her brother's execution. The friend was awakened by the loud sobs of Miss André, who said she had seen her brother made a prisoner. Her friend soothed her into quiet, and both fell asleep. Soon Miss André again awoke her friend, and said she had again seen her brother on trial as a spy. She described the scene with great particularity. Again she was quieted, and both fell asleep. Again she aroused her friend by screaming, " They are hanging him ! " They both made a memorandum of the affair. The next mail brought the sad news of André's execution at about the time when his sister, Mary Hannah, saw him in her vision.

Lieutenant André journeyed from England to Quebec, by way of Philadelphia. Why did he take this roundabout course ? He arrived at Philadelphia in September (1774), just after the first Continental Congress began its session there. His abilities as a keen observer of men and things were well known to General Carleton, the Governor of Canada, who arrived at Quebec from England while André was in Philadelphia. May not that astute officer have directed André, before he left England, to go to Philadelphia as a spy, to learn what he could of the condition of public affairs, and the temper of the people in the disturbed colonies, and especially the designs of the Continental Congress? From Philadelphia he went to New York and Boston, and thence by water to Quebec, everywhere traveling, without recognition, in citizen's dress. He undoubtedly carried to Carleton much valuable information which that wide-awake officer desired to know. André arrived at Quebec early in November.

A year later Lieutenant André was made a prisoner of war when Montgomery captured the fort at St. Johns, on the Sorel. " I have been taken a prisoner by the Americans," André wrote to Miss Seward, "and stripped of everything except the picture of Honora, which I concealed in my mouth. Preserving this, I yet think myself fortunate." He and his fellow-prisoners were taken first to Connecticut, and then to Lancaster and Carlisle in Pennsylvania. There he made many friends by his urbanity, his refined tastes, and his accomplishments. He taught the children of citizens the art of drawing in a free and easy style ; and he was a welcome guest in the higher social circles, was made a participant in all their pleasure-parties, and so added to their own enjoyments.

Toward the close of 1776 André was exchanged and joined the British army in New York, then commanded by General Howe. To that officer he presented a memoir on the existing war, which was very favorably received. He had kept a journal ever since he came to America, in which both pen and pencil were jointly employed in the delineation and description of everything of interest which came under his observation, and this furnished him with much material for his memoir. Howe was delighted with his young soldier, and as soon as a vacancy occurred he gave him the position of aide on the staff of General Grey, with the rank of captain. He was now fairly in the line of promotion which his signal abilities entitled him to receive.

André served with distinction as a staff-officer. He was the soul of the military social circle during the occupation of Philadelphia by the British army in the winter and spring of 1778. His pen, his pencil, and his brush, were continually busy in satirizing and caricaturing the " rebel " officers, or in dramatic exhibitions. He was a leader in all the social amusements of the army, the chief of which were theatrical performances. In these André was dramatist, actor, song-writer, and manager. He wrote prologues and localized plays, and was the chief manager of weekly balls. In a word, he was leader in setting on foot scenes of gayety and extravagance that were long remembered and lamented. André occupied the house of Dr. Franklin for several months. He carried away some valuable books.

Many of the young officers were scions of the British nobility, and possessed ample means for the gratification of any desire. The infection of demoralization that spread through the army and society was fearful. The army suffered much. Dr. Franklin said, " Howe did not take Philadelphia—Philadelphia took Howe." Cupid scattered his darts so widely and with such effect among the soldiers, that in the flight of the British army across New Jersey, on the evacuation of Philadelphia, fully six hundred soldiers deserted and returned to their sweethearts and lately married wives.

Many of the fair daughters of the Philadelphia loyalists were captivated by the young British officers. Among the latter was not one more fascinating than Major André, and no one was more welcome into the best society. He formed warm friendships with several leading families ; among others, that of Edward Shippen, one of the wealthiest and most cultivated citizens, whose youngest daughter married General Benedict Arnold.

Late in May, 1778, General Howe surrendered the command of the army into the hands of Sir Henry Clinton, and prepared to return to England. The officers of the army, who were very much attached to him, resolved to give him a spectacular parting entertainment which should eclipse in novelty and splendor anything ever seen in America. In the conception and preparation of the entertainment the genius of André, in all its phases, was brought into requisition. He designed the decorations, the costumes to be worn, even the ticket of admission to the show. The entertainment was called *Mischianza*—a medley. It was given at the country-seat of Thomas Wharton, a Philadelphia Quaker—a fine, stately mansion, with spacious grounds around it, standing near the present navy-yard.

CHAPTER II.

In a letter to his friend Miss Seward, dated Philadelphia, May 23, 1778, Major André gave the following account of the great *fête* in honor of General Howe :

" That our sentiments might be the more unreservedly and unequivocally known, it was resolved among us that we should give him as splendid an entertainment as the shortness of the time and our present situation would allow us. For the expenses the whole army would most cheerfully have contributed ; but it was requisite to draw the line somewhere, and twenty-two field-officers joined in a subscription adequate to a plan they meant to adopt. I know your curiosity will be raised on this occasion ; I shall, therefore, give you as particular an account of our *Mischianza** as I have been able to collect.

" From the name you will perceive that it was made up from a variety of entertainments. Four of the gentlemen subscribers were appointed managers—Sir John Wrottesley, Colonel O'Hara, Major Gardiner, and Montressor, the chief

THE MISCHIANZA TICKET.—(Drawn by Major André.)†

engineer. On the tickets of admission which they gave out for Monday, the 18th, was engraved, in a shield, a view of the sea, with the setting sun, and in a wreath the words

* This account was printed in the " Lady's Magazine," with which Miss Seward had a literary connection, in August, 1778.
† This is one half the size of the original.

'*Luceo discedens, aucto splendore resurgam.*' At top was the general's crest, with '*vive! vale!*' All round the shield ran a vignette, and various military trophies filled up the ground.*

" A grand regatta began the entertainment. It consisted of three divisions. In the first place was the *Ferret* galley, having on board several general officers and a number of ladies. In the center was the *Hussar* gal-

LADY'S HEAD-DRESS.
(Drawn by Major André.)

ley, with Sir William and Lord Howe, Sir Henry Clinton, the officers of their suite, and some ladies. The *Cornwallis* galley brought up the rear, having on board General Knyphausen and his suite, the British generals, and a party of ladies. On each quarter of these galleys, and forming their division, were five flat-boats, lined with green cloth, and filled with ladies and gentlemen. In front of the whole were three flat-boats, with a band of music in each. Six barges rowed about each flank, to keep off the swarm of boats that covered the river from side to side. The galleys were dressed out in a variety of colors and streamers, and on each flat-boat was displayed the flag of its own division. In the stream opposite the center of the city the *Fanny*,

---

* I copied this ticket from one of the originals in the Franklin Library, at Philadelphia, in 1848. It is attached, with drawings of a head-dress for the *Mischianza*, and a portrait of Captain Cathcart, a son of Lord Cathcart, to his manuscript " Annals of Philadelphia," deposited with this institution by the late John F. Watson, Esq. The designs for the ticket and the other sketches were made by André ; and a *silhouette* of Sir John Wrottesley, one of the managers, was cut by André. They were presented to Mr. Watson by Miss Craig, a participant in the *fête*. She was the chosen lady of the Second Knight of the Blended Rose. André's drawings for the costumes of the Ladies of the Blended Rose and Burning

armed ship, magnificently decorated, was placed at anchor; and at some distance ahead lay his Majesty's ship *Roebuck*, with the admiral's flag hoisted at the foretopmast-head. The transport ships, extending in a line the whole length of the town, appeared with colors flying and crowded with spectators, as were also the openings of the several wharves on the shore, exhibiting the most picturesque and enlivening scene the eye could desire. The rendezvous was at Knight's wharf, at the north end of the city." *

After giving an account of the aquatic procession down the river, André continues:

" The landing-place was the Old Fort, a little to the southward of the town,† fronting the building prepared for the reception of the company, about four hundred yards from the water by a gentle ascent. As soon as the general's barge was seen to push for the shore, a salute of seventeen guns was fired from the *Roebuck*, and, after some interval, by the same number by the *Vigilant*. The company, as they disembarked, arranged themselves into a line of procession, and advanced through an avenue formed by the two files of grenadiers, and a line of light horse supporting each file. This avenue led to a square lawn of two hundred and fifty yards on each side, lined with troops, and properly prepared for the exhibition of a tilt and tournament, according to the customs and ordinances of ancient chivalry. We proceeded

---

Mountain are preserved. The form was a polonaise, or a flowing robe of white silk, with a spangled pink sash and spangled shoes and stockings ; a veil spangled and trimmed with silver lace, and a towering head-dress of pearls and jewels. The Ladies of the Burning Mountain had their polonaises and white sashes bound with black. The engraving shows the style of the head-dress, copied from André's drawing.

* A little above Vine Street.
† A little below the present navy-yard.

through the center of the square. The music, consisting of all the bands of the army, moved in front. The managers, with favors of white and blue ribbons on their breasts, followed next in order. The general, admiral, and the rest of the company, succeeded promiscuously.

" In front of the building, bounding the view through a vista formed by two triumphal arches, erected at proper intervals in a line with the landing-place, two pavilions, with rows of benches rising one above another, and serving as the wings of the first triumphal arch, received the ladies, while the gentlemen ranged themselves in convenient order on each side. On the front seat of each pavilion were placed seven of the principal young ladies of the country, dressed in Turkish habits, and wearing on their turbans the favors with which they meant to reward the several knights who were to contend in their honor. These arrangements were scarcely made, when the sound of trumpets was heard at a distance; and a band of knights, dressed in ancient habits of white and red silk, and mounted on gray horses, richly caparisoned in trappings of the same colors, entered the lists, attended by their esquires on foot, in suitable apparel, in the following order :

" Four trumpeters, properly habited, their trumpets decorated with small pendent banners. A herald in his robes of ceremony ; on his tunic was the device of his band, two roses intertwined, with the motto—'*We droop when separated.*'

" Lord Cathcart, superbly mounted on a managed horse, appeared as chief of these knights; two young black slaves, with sashes and drawers of blue and white silk, wearing large silver clasps round their necks and arms, their breasts and shoulders bare, held his stirrups. On his right hand walked Captain Harard, and on his left Captain Brownlow, and his two esquires, the one bearing his lance, the other his shield. His device was Cupid riding on a lion; the motto —'*Surmounted by Love.*' His lordship appeared in honor of Miss Auchmuty.*

" Then came in order the knights of his band, each attended by his 'squire, bearing his lance and shield.

" First knight, Hon. Captain Cathcart,† in honor of Miss N. White.—'Squire, Captain Peters.—Device, á heart and sword ; motto—'*Love and Honor.*'

" Second knight, Lieutenant Bygrove, in honor of Miss Craig.—'Squire, Lieutenant Nichols.—Device, Cupid tracing a circle ; motto—'*Without End.*'

" Third knight, Captain André, in honor of Miss P. Chew.‡—'Squire, Lieutenant André.#—Device, two game-cocks fighting ; motto—'*No rival.*'

" Fourth knight, Captain Horneck, in honor of Miss N. Redmond.—'Squire, Lieutenant Talbot.—Device, a burning heart ; motto—'*Absence can not extinguish.*'

---

* Miss Auchmuty was the only English maiden present. She was about to become the bride of Captain Montressor, the chief engineer. Watson says there were not more than fifty unmarried American ladies present ; the rest were all married.

† Captain Cathcart, the son of Lord Cathcart, married a daughter of Andrew Eliot, once a collector of customs at Philadelphia. The young officer had been making love most vehemently to Miss Eliot all winter. She was pretty, lively, and well educated. The captain wrote her many letters, avowing his love for her, but much of his conduct seems to have been mere coquetry. Miss Eliot was in earnest, and received his attentions and his letters as genuine tokens of his love. When it became evident that he meant to deceive her, her father laid his letters before Sir Henry Clinton, of whose military family young Cathcart was a member. Clinton advised the young man to marry Miss Eliot. Cathcart wished to postpone it until the end of the war. Clinton told him he had gone so far that he must marry her speedily or leave his family. They were married in April, 1779. She was afterward " Lady Cathcart," and appeared at court when her husband became an earl.

‡ A daughter of Chief-Justice Chew.

A brother of Captain André, then nineteen years of age. After André's death, he was knighted by the king.

"Fifth knight, Captain Mathews, in honor of Miss Bond.
—'Squire, Lieutenant Hamilton.—Device, a winged heart;
motto—' *Each fair by turns.*'

"Sixth knight, Lieutenant Sloper, in honor of Miss M.
Shippen.*—'Squire, Lieutenant Brown.—Device, a heart and
sword ; motto—' *Honor and the fair.*'"

THE JOUST AT THE TOURNAMENT.

After they had made the circuit of the square, and saluted the ladies as they passed before the pavilion, they
ranged themselves in a line with that in which were the

---

* Afterward the wife of Benedict Arnold.

ladies of their device ; and their herald (Mr. Beaumont) advancing into the center of the square, after a flourish of trumpets, proclaimed the following challenge :

" The Knights of the Blended Rose, by me, their herald, proclaim and assert that the Ladies of the Blended Rose excel in wit, beauty, and every accomplishment, those of the whole world ; and should any knight or knights be so hardy as to dispute or deny it, they are ready to enter the lists with them, and maintain their assertions by deeds of arms, according to the laws of ancient chivalry."

At the third repetition of this challenge, the sound of trumpets was heard from the opposite side of the square ; and another herald, with four trumpeters, dressed in black-and-orange, galloped into the lists. He was met by the Herald of the Blended Rose, and, after a short parley, they both advanced in front of the pavilions, when the black herald (Lieutenant Moore) ordered his trumpets to sound, and thus proclaimed defiance to the challenge in the following words :

" The Knights of the Burning Mountain present themselves here, not to contest by words, but to disprove by deeds, the vainglorious assertions of the Knights of the Blended Rose, and enter these lists to maintain that the Ladies of the Burning Mountain are not excelled in beauty, virtue, or accomplishments, by any in the universe."

He then returned to the part of the barrier through which he had entered, and shortly afterward the Black Knights, attended by their 'squires, rode into the lists in the following order :

" Four trumpeters preceding the herald, on whose tunic was represented a mountain sending forth flames ; motto— *''I burn forever.'*

"Captain Watson, of the Guards, as chief, dressed in a magnificent suit of black-and-orange silk, and mounted on a black managed horse, with trappings of the same color with his own dress, appeared in honor of Miss Franks. He was attended in the same manner with Lord Cathcart. Captain Scott bore his lance and Lieutenant Lytton his shield. The device, a heart, with a wreath of flowers ; motto—' *Love and glory.*'

" First knight, Lieutenant Underwood, in honor of Miss S. Shippen.—'Squire, Ensign Haserkam.—Device, a pelican feeding her young ; motto—' *For those I love.*'

" Second knight, Lieutenant Wingard, in honor of Miss R. P. Shippen.—'Squire, Captain Boscawen.—Device, a bay-leaf ; motto—' *Unchangeable.*'

" Third knight, Lieutenant Deleval, in honor of Miss B. Bond.—'Squire, Captain Thorne.—Device, a heart, aimed at by several arrows, and struck by one ; motto—' *Only one pierces me.*'

" Fourth knight, Monsieur Montluissent (Lieutenant of the Hessian Chasseurs), in honor of Miss B. Redman.— 'Squire, Captain Campbell. — Device, a sunflower turning toward the sun ; motto—' *Je vise à vous.*'

" Fifth knight, Lieutenant Hobart, in honor of Miss S. Chew.—'Squire, Lieutenant Briscoe.—Device, Cupid piercing a coat-of-mail with his arrow ; motto—' *Proof to all but love.*'

" Sixth knight, Brigade-Major Tarleton, in honor of Miss W. Smith.—'Squire, Captain Heart.—Device, a light dragoon ; motto—' *Swift, vigilant, and bold.*'

" After they had rode round the lists, and made their obeisance to the ladies, they drew up, fronting the White Knights ; and the chief of them having thrown down his gauntlet, the Chief of the Black Knights directed his esquire to take it up. The knights then received their lances from their esquires, fixed their shields on their left arms, and, making a general salute to each other by a very graceful movement of their lances, turned round to take their career, and, encountering in full gallop, shivered their spears. In the second and third encounter they discharged their pistols. In the fourth they fought with swords. At length the two chiefs, spurring forward into the center, engaged furiously in single combat, till the marshal of the field (Major Gwyne) rushed in between the chiefs and declared that the Fair Damsels of the Blended Rose and Burning Mountain were perfectly satisfied with the proofs of love and the signal feats of valor given by their respective knights; and commanded them, as they prized the future favors of their mistresses, that they would instantly desist from further combat. Obedience being paid by the chiefs to the order, they joined their respective bands. The White Knights and their attendants filed off to the left, the Black Knights to the right, and, after passing each other at the lower side of the quadrangle, moved up alternately till they approached the pavilion of the ladies, where they gave a general salute.

" A passage being now opened between the pavilions, the knights, preceded by their 'squires and the bands of music, rode through the first triumphal arch and arranged themselves to the right and left. This arch was erected in honor of Lord Howe. It presented two fronts, in the Tuscan order; the pediment was adorned with various naval trophies, and at the top was a figure of Neptune, with a trident in his right hand. In a niche on each side stood a sailor with a drawn cutlass. Three plumes of feathers were placed on the summit of each wing, and on the entablature was this

inscription : '*Laus illi debetur, et a me gratia major.*' The
interval between the two arches was an avenue three hundred feet long and thirty-four broad. It was lined on each
side with a file of troops; and the colors of all the army,
planted at proper distances, had a beautiful effect in diversi-
fying the scene.

"Between these colors the knights and 'squires took
their stations. The bands continued to play several pieces
of martial music. The company moved forward in procession, with the ladies in the Turkish habits in front: as
these passed they were saluted by their knights, who then
dismounted and joined them ; and in this order we were all
conducted into a garden that fronted the house, through the
second triumphal arch dedicated to the general. This arch
was also built in the Tuscan order. On the interior part of
the pediment were painted a Plume of Feathers and various
military trophies. At the top stood the figure of Fame, and
on the entablature these words—'*I, bone, quo virtuo tua le
vocet ; I pede fausto.*' On the right-hand pillar was placed a
bomb-shell, and on the left a flaming heart. The front next
the house was adorned with preparations for a fire-work.

"From the garden we ascended a flight of steps covered
with carpets, which led into a spacious hall ; the panels,
painted in imitation of Sienna marble,* inclosing portions
of white marble ; the surbase and all below were black. In
this hall, and in the adjoining apartments, were prepared
tea, lemonade, and other cooling liquors, to which the com-

---

* The painting was done in distemper upon canvas, in the manner of theatrical
scene-painting.   André was assisted in his art-work by Captain Oliver De Lancey,
of New York, an energetic leader of loyalists.   He married a daughter of David
Franks.   She was active in the *Mischianza* affair.   Her sister married Colonel
Johnson, of the British army, who was in command at Stony Point, on the Hudson,
when it was captured by General Wayne in the summer of 1779.

pany seated themselves ; during which time the knights
came in, and on the knee received their favors from their
respective ladies. One of these rooms was afterward appropriated to the use of the Pharaoh table. As you entered it
you saw, in a panel over the chimney, a cornucopia, exuber-
antly filled with flowers of the richest colors. Over the
door, as you went out, another presented itself, shrunk, re-
versed, and emptied.

" From these apartments we were conducted up to a ball-
room, decorated in a light, elegant style of painting. The
ground was a pale blue, paneled with a small gold bead, and
in the interior filled with dropping festoons of flowers in
their natural colors. Below the surface the ground was of
rose-pink, with drapery festooned in blue. These decorations were heightened by eighty-five mirrors, decked with
rose-pink silk ribbons and artificial flowers ; and in the inter-
mediate spaces were thirty-four branches with wax-lights,
ornamented in a similar manner. On the same floor were
four drawing-rooms, with sideboards of refreshments, decorated and lighted in the same style and taste as the ball-
room.

" The ball was opened by the knights and their ladies,
and the dances continued till ten o'clock, when the windows
were thrown open, and a magnificent bouquet of rockets began the fire-works. These were planned by Captain Montressor, the chief-engineer, and consisted of twenty different
exhibitions, displayed under his directions with the happiest
success and in the highest style of beauty. Toward the conclusion the interior part of the triumphal arch was illumi-
nated amid an uninterrupted flight of rockets and bursting
balloons. The military trophies on each side assumed a variety of transparent colors. The shell and flaming heart on

the wings sent forth Chinese fountains, succeded by fire-works. Fame appeared at the top, spangled with stars, and from her trumpet blowing the following device in letters of light : '*Les lauriers sont immortels.*' A *sauteur* of rockets bursting from the pediment concluded the *feu d'artifice.*

"At twelve supper was announced, and large folding-doors, hitherto artfully concealed, being suddenly thrown open, discovered a magnificent saloon of two hundred and ten feet by forty, and twenty-two in height, with three al-coves on each side, which served for sideboards. The ceil-ing was the segment of a circle, and the sides were painted of a light straw-color, with vine-leaves and festoon-flowers, some in a bright and some in a darkish green. Fifty-six large pier-glasses, ornamented with green silk, artificial flowers, and ribbons ; a hundred branches with three lights in each, trimmed in the same manner as the mirrors ; eighteen lus-ters, each with twenty-four lights, suspended from the ceil-ing, and ornamented as the branches ; three hundred wax-tapers disposed along the supper-tables ; four hundred and thirty covers ; twelve hundred dishes ; twenty-four black slaves, in Oriental dresses, with silver collars and bracelets, ranged in two lines and bending to the ground as the gen-eral and admiral approached the saloon—all these, forming together the most brilliant assemblage of gay objects, and appearing at once as we entered by an easy ascent, exhibited a *coup d'œil* beyond description magnificent.

"Toward the end of the supper the Herald of the Blended Rose, in his habit of ceremony, attended by his trumpeters, entered the saloon, and proclaimed the king's health, the queen and royal family, the army and navy, with their respective commanders, the knights and their ladies, and the ladies in general. Each of these toasts was followed by a flourish of music. After supper we returned to the ball-room and continued to dance until four o'clock."

CHAPTER III.

THE *Mischianza* was severely criticised in Great Britain and America, as an undeserved compliment to an incompetent officer. Howe was an indolent procrastinator, and fond of sensual indulgence ; and he had not only effected nothing of importance for his country in America, but had hindered more competent men. He was charged by Galloway, a Philadelphia Tory then in London, with "a vanity and presumption unparalleled in history, after his indolence and wretched blunders," in accepting from a few officers "a triumph more magnificent than would have become the conqueror of America, without the consent of his sovereign or approbation of his country."

It is asserted that at Philadelphia Howe was openly licentious, kept a mistress, loved his bottle inordinately, and engaged secretly in business transactions for his own gain, similar to those with which Benedict Arnold was charged, and caused him to be reprimanded by order of Congress. Horace Walpole said, "He returned to England richer in money than in laurels." Another said, "The only bays he possessed were those that drew his carriage " ; and still another, that "he has given America to the Americans." And yet staid men, as well as romantic enthusiasts like André, did not hesitate to award him honors which only great heroes and most virtuous men deserve. André even wrote a fulsome poetic address to be read to Howe during the *fête.*

The general exercised good sense by forbidding its utter-
ance.

The extreme folly of the *Mischianza*, under the peculiar
circumstances, was deplored by sensible men in and out of
the army. When an old British major of artillery, in Philadelphia, was asked by a young person what was the distinction between the "Knights of the Burning Mountain" and
the "Knights of the Blended Rose," the veteran replied:
"The 'Knights of the Burning Mountain' are tom-fools, and
the 'Knights of the Blended Rose' are damned fools! I know
of no other distinction between them." The old soldier,
though a Briton, greatly admired Washington. Placing a
hand upon each knee, he added, in a tone of deep mortifica-
tion, "What will Washington think of this?"

Just one month after this grand show at Philadelphia, a far
grander and more important spectacle was exhibited at that
city. It was the sudden flight of the whole British army from
the town, across the Delaware and over New Jersey, eagerly
pressing toward New York; also the speedy entrance of Continental troops into Philadelphia, and the return of Congress.

Sir Henry Clinton, now in chief command of the British
army, was making preparations for a vigorous campaign,
when orders came from the ministers to evacuate Philadelphia at once, to prevent a blockade of the army and navy
on the Delaware by a French fleet under D'Estaing, then on
its way to America. Clinton obeyed. Washington, with his
recuperated army at Valley Forge, pursued and overtook
the fugitives near Monmouth Court-House. There, on a
very hot Sunday in June (28th), a sanguinary but indecisive
battle was fought. That night Clinton secretly stole away
with his whole force (while the wearied Americans slept on
their arms), and escaped to New York.

Lord Howe had scarcely left the Capes of the Delaware, when D'Estaing appeared. Howe sailed for New York, and anchored his fleet in Raritan Bay. D'Estaing's larger vessels could not enter the shallow waters of the bay, and sailed away for Rhode Island, to assist American troops in expelling the British from that domain. A storm dispersed the two fleets. The attempt at expulsion was a failure. Clinton sailed with four thousand troops to strengthen British power on Rhode Island. Thence he sent General Grey on a marauding expedition to New Bedford and its vicinity, André accompanied him, and afterward wrote an amusing poem, to the tune of " Yankee Doodle," entitled " Yankee Doodle's Expedition to Rhode Island."* He also wrote a poem, in eighteen stanzas, giving an amusing account of a duel between Christopher Gadsden, of South Carolina, and General Robert Howe, of the Continental army. This poem may be found in Sargent's " Life and Career of Major An-dré." Other poems, evidently from André's pen, ridiculing the " rebels," frequently appeared in Rivington's " Royal Gazette," until the tragedy that ended his life in the fall of 1780.

Late in 1778 General Grey returned to England, when André took the position of aide to General Clinton, with the rank of provincial major. He evinced such eminent clerical and executive ability that early in 1779 he was made deputy adjutant-general of the British forces in America.

The city of New York continued to be the headquarters of the British army until the close of the war. Clinton made his quarters at No. 1 Broadway, a spacious house, with a

---

* This poem, with explanatory notes, may be found in Frank Moore's " Ballads of the Revolution."

garden extending to the Hudson River. He also occupied
the fine Beekman mansion at Turtle Bay as a summer residence.

The British officers made the city a theatre of great
gayety. They were continually engaged in every kind of
amusement, to while away their time when not on active
duty. In these amusements Major André was ever conspicuous, especially in dramatic performances ; and there he
freely indulged his love for good-natured satirical writing.
He wrote much for Rivington's " Gazette " in prose and
verse—political squibs, satires, and lampoons—the "rebels "
and their doings being his chief theme.

It was at No. 1 Broadway that André wrote his best-
known poem, " The Cow-Chase," in imitation of "Chevy
Chase." There he also wrote his most elaborate prose com-
position, " A Dream." This he read aloud at a social gathering, and it was published in Rivington's paper. In his
position on Clinton's staff he was able to exercise his ever-
kindly disposition toward the unfortunate, and never left
unimproved an opportunity to do so.

Major André was with Sir Henry Clinton on an expedition up the Hudson in May, 1779, when the British captured the American post of Stony Point, and Fort Lafayette,
on Verplanck's Point, opposite. When the batteries of Fort
Lafayette were silenced, André was sent to receive the surrender of the garrison and the works. A few weeks later he
wrote a friendly letter to Margaret Shippen (then the wife
of General Benedict Arnold), in whose family the major had
been a great favorite while in Philadelphia. The letter
was dated " Headquarters, New York, the 16th of August,
1779." He offered to do some "shopping " in New York
for Mrs. Arnold, saying :

" It would make me very happy to become useful to you here. You know the *Mischianza* made me a complete milliner. Should you not have received supplies for your fullest equipment for that department, I shall be glad to enter into the whole detail of cap-wire, needles, gauze, etc., and to the best of my ability render you in these trifles services from which I hope you would infer a zeal to be further employed. I beg you would present my best respects to your sisters, to the Miss Chews, and to Mrs. Shippen and Mrs. Chew.

" I have the honor to be, with the greatest regard, madam, your most obedient and most humble servant,

" JOHN ANDRÉ."

General Arnold had been made military governor of Philadelphia after the American troops and Congress repossessed it. He lived most extravagantly. He kept a coach-and-four, with a coachman in livery ; gave sumptuous dinner parties, and charmed the gayer portion of Philadelphia society by his princely display. He was keenly watched by men who knew his character well, or envied his success as a soldier, and he was hated by persons in exalted positions for his many bad qualities. Among the latter was General Joseph Reed, then President of the Executive Council of Pennsylvania. Early in 1779 that Council submitted to Congress charges against Arnold of being guilty of malfeasance in office. Congress referred the charges to a committee of inquiry, whose report exculpated the general from all criminality in the matter charged against him.

Arnold promptly asked Congress to investigate the charges. He regarded this report of the committee as a vindication of his character ; but he immediately urged

Congress to act speedily upon the report. Instead of doing so, the report was referred to a joint committee of Congress and the Executive Council of Pennsylvania. They passed a resolution to refer some of the charges to a court-martial, to be appointed by Washington. When the charges were so referred, Arnold was indignant, but was compelled to submit. He urged prompt action, but a court-martial to try him was not convened until December following. They gave their decision on the 26th of January, 1780. The accused was acquitted of several of the charges, and of "all intentional wrong" in the whole matter of the other charges; but it was decided that, for "imprudent and improper conduct," he should be reprimanded by the commander-in-chief. This was done in the most delicate manner by Washington; but, as it implied a stigma upon his character, Arnold was exceedingly indignant. This act doubtless stimulated him in his treasonable undertaking, in which he appears to have been already engaged for fully nine months. Dr. Sparks says: " He [Arnold] had already made secret advances to the enemy under a feigned name, intending to square his conduct according to circumstances; and prepared, if the court decided against him, to seek revenge at any hazard."

There appears to be clear evidence that overtures were first made by the other side, probably by Beverly Robinson,* to whom is attributed a letter given by Marbois, who was attached to the French legation at Philadelphia.† Be that as it may, it is known that correspondence between General Arnold and Sir Henry Clinton began so early as the spring

---

* Beverly Robinson was a gentleman of fortune, a son-in-law of Frederick Phillipse, proprietor of Phillipse Manor on the Hudson, and a very active Tory.
† See a copy of this letter in the " Life and Career of John André," by Winthrop Sargent, p. 447.

of 1779. Arnold wrote in a disguised hand, and under the assumed name of "Gustavus." The tenor of the correspondence was of a commercial character, so as to mislead others.

After the exchange of two or three letters, and with the impression that "Gustavus" was an officer of high rank in . the American army, Clinton committed the task of carrying

FAC-SIMILE OF ARNOLD'S DISGUISED HANDWRITING.

on the correspondence to Major André, who wrote over the signature of " John Anderson," in a slightly disguised hand. Not doubting that "Gustavus" was General Arnold, André probably wrote the letter to Mrs. Arnold in August for the

FAC-SIMILE OF ANDRÉ'S DISGUISED HANDWRITING.

purpose of making clear to her husband the name and character of "John Anderson " by means of his handwriting :

Major André was with Sir Henry Clinton at the siege

and capture of Charleston in the spring of 1780, and there
is clear evidence that he played the part of a spy in that
tragedy. It is asserted that Edward Shrewsberry, a respectable citizen of Charleston, but a suspected Tory, was ill at
his house on East Bay during the siege. His Whig brother,
who belonged to the American army, frequently visited
him. He saw at his Tory brother's house, on several occa-
sions, a young man clad in homespun, who was introduced
to him as a Virginian, also belonging to the patriot army.
After the capitulation, and the British were in possession of
the city, the Continental soldier saw at the house of his sick
brother the same young man, but in different apparel, who
was introduced to him as Major André, of the British army.
His brother afterward confessed that the major and the
homespun-clad young "Virginian" were one and the same
man. To another visitor this young man in homespun was
introduced by Shrewsberry as "a back-country man who
had brought down cattle for the garrison." He was afterward informed that the cattle-driver was Major André.

If these assertions be true—and there is no reason for
doubting their truth—Major André did not hesitate, when
an occasion offered, to play the part of a spy for the benefit
of his king and country. Six months afterward, when circumstances had placed him in that position, and he was a
prisoner, he expressed, in a letter to Washington, a desire to
rescue himself from "an imputation of having assumed a
mean character for treacherous purposes or self-interest."

In the early autumn of 1780 Major André was made adjutant-general of the British forces in America. He was then
busy in consummating the intrigue and conspiracy with Arnold. The time had arrived when it had become necessary
to bring matters to a head—to settle upon a definite plan and

time for action, terms, etc. Arnold had, at his own earnest solicitation, been appointed to the command at West Point and its dependencies in August, and had resolved to surrender that strong post into the hands of the enemies of his country. It was an object of covetous desire on the part of the British, for the possession of it would open a free communication between New York and Canada, which they had been endeavoring to secure ever since the invasion of Burgoyne in 1777. The subject of the surrender of West Point was the burden of the correspondence between Arnold and André early in September.

At midsummer, 1780, an occasion drew from Major André's pen his most notable satirical poem, in imitation, in structure and metre, of the famous old British ballad, "Chevy Chase." It appears to have been written for the twofold purpose of gratifying his own quick perception of the ludicrous and to retaliate in kind the satirical attacks of Whig writers upon him and his friends. The occasion was an expedition in July against a block-house on the west bank of the Hudson, three or four miles below Fort Lee, at the base of the Palisades, which was occupied by a British picket of seventy men—loyal refugees—for the protection of some wood-cutters and the neighboring Tories.

On Bergen Neck, not far from the block-house, were a large number of cattle and horses within reach of the British foragers who might go out from the fort at Paulus' Hook (now Jersey City). Washington sent General Wayne with horse and foot—less than two thousand men—to storm the block-house and to drive the cattle within the American lines. Wayne sent the cavalry under Major Henry Lee ("Legion Harry," father of the late General Robert E. Lee, of the Confederate army), to perform the latter duty, while

6 .

he, with three regiments, marched against the block-house
with four pieces of light artillery. A brief but sharp skirmish
ensued. The assailants were compelled to retire, and Wayne
returned to camp with a large number of cattle driven by
the dragoons. The failure to capture the block-house was
attributed to the ineffectualness of the small cannons.

The "Cow-Chase" was published in Rivington's "Gazette," the last canto on the day of the author's arrest as a
spy at Tarrytown. He made copies of the poem for his
friends. Of one of these, belonging to the late Rev. Dr.
Sprague, of Albany, I was permitted, in 1849, to make the
following copy of the poem given in the next chapter; also
the fac-simile given of the last stanza of the poem in the
handwriting of Major André.

CHAPTER IV.

COW-CHASE.

BY MAJOR JOHN ANDRÉ.

ELIZABETHTOWN, *August* 1, 1780.

CANTO 1.

To drive the kine, one summer's morn,
The tanner * took his way :
The calf shall rue that is unborn
The jumbling of that day.

And Wayne descending steers shall know,
And tauntingly deride,
And call to mind, in ev'ry low,
The tanning of his hide.

---

* André seems to have been impressed with the idea that the occupation of
General Wayne, the leader of the expedition, was that of a tanner in his early life.
A few foot-notes were made to the poem when it was published in England.
These are here placed in italics. The remainder are by the author of this volume.

Let Bergen cows still ruminate
  Unconscious in the stall,
What mighty means were used to get,
  And lose them after all.

For many heroes bold and brave '
  From New Bridge and Tapaan,
And those that drink Passaic's wave,
  And those that eat soupaan ; *

And sons of distant Delaware,
  And still remoter Shannon,
And Major Lee with horses rare,
  And Proctor with his cannon—

All wondrous proud in arms they came !
  What hero could refuse
To tread the rugged path to fame,
  Who had a pair of shoes ? †

At six the host, with sweating buff,
  Arrived at Freedom's Pole, ‡
When Wayne, who thought he'd time enough,
  Thus speechified the whole :

" O ye whom glory doth unite,
  Who Freedom's cause espouse,
Whether the wing that's doomed to fight,
  Or that to drive the cows ;

" Ere yet you tempt your further way,
  Or into action come,
Hear, soldiers, what I have to say,
  And take a pint of rum.#

" Intemperate valor then will string
  Each nervous arm the better,

---

* *A hasty-pudding made of the meal of Indian corn.*
  † This is in allusion to the fact that many of the American soldiers, at that time, were without shoes or stockings.
  ‡ *Freedom's, i. e., liberty-pole—a long stick stuck in the ground.*
  # Rum was the usual kind of spirituous liquor that formed a portion of the rations of the soldiers.

So all the land shall IO ! sing,
    And read the gen'ral's letter. *

" Know that some paltry refugees,
    Whom I've a mind to fight,
Are playing h—l among the trees
    That grow on yonder height !

" Their fort and block-house we'll level,
    And deal a horrid slaughter;
We'll drive the scoundrels to the devil,
    And ravish wife and daughter.

" I under cover of th' attack,
    Whilst you are all at blows,
From English Neighb'rhood and Tinack
    Will drive away the cows.

" For well you know the latter is
    The serious operation,
And fighting with the refugees †
    Is only—demonstration."

His daring words from all the crowd
    Such great applause did gain,
That every man declared aloud
    For serious work with—Wayne.

Then from the cask of rum once more
    They took a heavy gill,
When one and all they loudly swore
    They'd fight upon the hill.

But here—the Muse has not a strain
    Befitting such great deeds :
" Hurra," they cried, " hurra for Wayne !"
    ˙ And, shouting—did their needs.

---

* In his letter to Congress (July 26, 1780) concerning this expedition, Washington spoke of the American cannons being "too light to penetrate the logs of which
it [the block-house] was constructed." He also attributed the great loss of the
Americans in that attack to the "intemperate valor" of the men. André exercised
a poetical license in putting these words into the mouth of Wayne before the
occurrence.
    † Loyalists expelled from the American lines.

CANTO II.

Near his meridian pomp the sun
　　Had journeyed from th' horizon,
When fierce the dusky tribe moved on,
　　Of heroes drunk as poison.

The sounds confused, of boasting oaths,
　　Re-echoed through the wood :
Some vowed to sleep in dead men's clothes,
　　And some to swim in blood.

At Irvine's nod, 'twas fine to see
　　The left prepared to fight,
The while the drovers, Wayne and Lee
　　Drew off upon the right.

Which Irvine 'twas Fame don't relate,
　　Nor can the Muse assist her—
Whether 'twas he that cocks a hat,
　　Or he that gives a glister.

For greatly one was signalized,
　　That fought at Chestnut Hill,
And Canada immortalized
　　The vender of the pill.*

Yet the attendance upon Proctor
　　They both might have to boast of ;
For there was business for the doctor,
　　And hats to be disposed of.

Let none uncandidly infer
　　That Stirling wanted spunk,
The self-made Peer† had sure been there,
　　But that the Peer was drunk.

---

* *One of the Irvines was a hatter, the other was a physician.* It was probably the latter—Dr. William Irvine—who was in this expedition, for he was then in command of the Second Pennsylvania Regiment. He had been a captain in Canada about two years. Brigadier-General Irvine was made a prisoner at Chestnut Hill, near Philadelphia, in December, 1777.

† William Alexander, Lord Stirling, was a general in the Continental army. He had been frustrated in obtaining a Scottish estate and peerage to which he was clearly entitled. He assumed the title as a right.

But turn we to the Hudson's banks,
    Where stood the modest train,
With purpose firm, though slender ranks,
    Nor cared a pin for Wayne.

For then the unrelenting hand
    Of rebel fury drove,
And tore from ev'ry genial hand
    Of friendship and of love.

And some within a dungeon's gloom,
    By mock tribunals laid,
Had waited long a cruel doom,
    Impending o'er their head.

Here one bewails a brother's fate,
    There one a sire demands,
Cut off, alas ! before their date,
    By ignominious hands.

And silvered grandsires here appeared
    In deep distress serene,
Of reverend manners that declared
    The better days they'd seen.

Oh ! cursed rebellion, these are thine,
    Thine are these tales of woe ;
Shall at thy dire, insatiate shrine
    Blood never cease to flow ?

And now the foe began to lead
    His forces to the attack ; ·
Balls whistling unto balls succeed,
    And make the block-house crack.

No shot could pass, if you will take
    The gen'ral's word for true ; *
But 'tis a d——le mistake,
    For ev'ry shot went through.

---

* General Wayne reported that, owing to the lightness of his field-pieces, the
shot did not penetrate the logs of the block-house.

The firmer as the rebels pressed,
The loyal heroes stand ;
Virtue had nerved each honest breast,
And industry each hand.

In valor's frenzy, Hamilton *
Rode like a soldier big,
And Secretary Harrison †
With pen stuck in his wig.

But, lest chieftain Washington
Should mourn them in the mumps,‡
The fate of Withington to shun,
They fought *behind* the stumps. #

But ah ! Thaddeus Posset, why
Should thy poor soul elope ?
And why should Titus Hooper die—
Ah ! die without a rope ?

Apostate Murphy, thou to whom
Fair Shela ne'er was cruel ;
In death shalt hear her mourn thy doom,
"Och ! would ye die, my jewel ? "

Thee, Nathan Pumpkin, I lament,
Of melancholy fate ;
The gray goose, stolen as he went,
In his heart's blood was wet.

---

* *Vide Lee's trial.* General Charles Lee, in his testimony at his trial by court-martial, after the battle of Monmouth, spoke of " Colonel Hamilton flourishing his sword " after delivering a message from Washington on the battle-field, and saying, " ' I will stay, and we will all die here on this spot.' I could not but be surprised," said Lee, " at his expression, but observed him much fluttered, and in a sort of frenzy of valor."

† Richard Harrison, Washington's secretary.

‡ *A disorder prevalent in the rebel lines.*

The merit of these lines, which is doubtless very great, can only be felt by true connoisseurs conversant in ancient song. In " Chevy Chase " occurs the stanza :

" For Witherington needs must I wayle,
As one in doleful dumps ;
For when his legges were smitten off,
He fought upon his stumps."

Now, as the fight was further fought,
  And balls began to thicken,
The fray assumed, the gen'rals thought,
  The color of a licking.

Yet undismayed, the chiefs command,
  And, to redeem the day,
Cry, "Soldiers, charge!" They hear, they stand—
  They turn and run away!

CANTO III.

Not all delights the bloody spear,
  Or horrid din of battle;
There are, I'm sure, who'd like to hear
  A word about the rattle.

The chief whom we beheld of late
  Near Schralenberg haranguing,
At Yan Van Poop's * unconscious sat
  Of Irvine's hearty banging;

While valiant Lee, with courage wild,
  Most bravely did oppose
The tears of women and of child,
  Who begged he'd leave the cows.

But Wayne, of sympathizing heart,
  Requirèd a relief
Not all the blessings could impart
  Of battle or of beef.

For now a prey to female charms,
  His soul took more delight in
A lovely Hamadryad's † arms,
  Than cow-driving or fighting.

A nymph, the refugees had drove
  Far from her native tree,
Just happened to be on the move,
  When up came Wayne and Lee.

* *Who kept a dram-shop.*   † *A deity of the woods.*

She in mad Anthony's fierce eye
　　The hero saw portrayed,
And, all in tears, she took him by
　　The bridle of his jade.*

" Hear," said the nymph, " O great commander,
　　No human lamentations ;
The trees you see them cutting yonder
　　Are all my near relations.

" And I, forlorn, implore thine aid
　　To free the sacred grove ;
So shall thy prowess be repaid
　　With an immortal's love."

Now some, to prove she was a goddess,
　　Said this enchanting fair
Had late retired from the *Bodies* †
　　In all the pomp of war ;

That drums and merry fifes had played
　　To honor her retreat,
And Cunningham ‡ himself conveyed
　　The lady through the street.

Great Wayne, by soft compassion swayed,
　　To no inquiry stoops,
But takes the fair, afflicted maid
　　Right into Yan Van Poop's.

So Roman Anthony, they say,
　　Disgraced the imperial banner,
And for a gypsy lost a day,
　　Like Anthony the tanner.

The Hamadryad had but half
　　Received redress from Wayne,
When drums and colors, cow and calf,
　　Came down the road amain.

---

* *A New England name for a horse, mare, or gelding.*

† *A cant appellation given among the soldiers to the corps that has the honor to guard his Majesty's person*—a body-guard,

‡ William Cunningham, the veteran provost-marshal at New York.

All in a cloud of dust were seen
    The sheep, the horse, the goat,
The gentle heifer, ass obscene,
    The yearling, and the shoat.

And pack-horses with fowls came by,
    Befeathered on each side,
Like Pegasus, the horse that I
    And other poets ride.

Sublime upon the stirrups rose
    The mighty Lee behind,
And drove the terror-smitten cows
    Like chaff before the wind !

But sudden see the woods above
    Pour down another corps,
All helter-skelter in a drove,
    Like that I sung before.

Irvine and terror in the van
    Came flying all abroad,
And cannon, colors, horse, and man,
    Ran tumbling to the road.

Still as he fled, 'twas Irvine's cry,
    And his example too :
" Run on, my merry men, all—for why ? "
    The shot will not go through.

Five refugees, 'tis true, were found
    Stiff on the block-house floor ;
But then, 'tis thought, the shot went round,
    And in at the back door !

As when two kennels in the street,
    Swelled with a recent rain,
In gushing streams together meet,
    And seek the neighboring drain—

So meet these dung-born tribes in one,
    As swift in their career,
And so to New Bridge they ran on,
    But all the cows got clear.

Poor Parson Caldwell, all in wonder,
Saw the returning train,
And mourned to Wayne the lack of plunder,
For them to steal again.*

For 'twas his right to seize the spoil, and
To share with each commander,
As he had done at Staten Island
With frost-bit Alexander.†

In his dismay, the frantic priest
Began to grow prophetic,
You had swore, to see his lab'ring breast,
He'd taken an emetic !

" I view a future day," said he,
" Brighter than this day dark is,
And you shall see what you shall see,
Ha ! ha ! one pretty marquis ; ‡

" And he shall come to Paulus Hook,#
And great achievements think on,
And make a bow and take a look,
Like Satan over Lincoln.

" And all the land around shall glory
To see the Frenchmen caper,
And pretty Susan ‖ tell the story
In the next Chatham paper."

---

* Rev. James Caldwell, an earnest Whig of New Jersey, and pastor of a church at Connecticut Farms. His wife had been shot by a newly enlisted soldier in her own house, when the British, under Knyphausen, made a raid upon Springfield in 1778.

† *Calling himself, because he was ordered not to do it, Earl of Stirling, though no sterling earl.* (See foot-note, page 71.) In a winter expedition to Staten Island a larger proportion of his soldiers were frost-bitten.

‡ *Lafayette.*

Now Jersey City, where the British had a redoubt. This Major Henry Lee surprised, in August, 1779, and carried away one hundred and fifty-nine of the garrison prisoners.

‖ Mrs. Susannah Livingston, a daughter of Governor William Livingston, of New Jersey, who was suspected of political authorship.

This solemn prophecy, of course,
    Gave all much consolation ;
Except to Wayne, who lost his horse
    Upon the great occasion—

His horse that carried all his prog,
    His military speeches,
His corn-stalk whisky for his grog—
    Blue stockings and brown breeches.

And now I've closed my epic strain,
    I tremble as I show it,
Lest this same warrio-drover, Wayne,
    Should ever catch the poet.*

And now ▭▭ I've clos'd my Epic strain,
I tremble as I show it,
Lest this same warrio-drover Wayne
Should ever catch the Poet.

Finis

FAC-SIMILE OF THE LAST STANZA OF THE COW-CHASE.

CHAPTER V.

WE have seen that Arnold, at his own earnest solicitation, had been appointed to the command of West Point
in August, 1780. It was then known to Sir Henry Clinton

---

* It so happened that when André was taken to Tappaan he was delivered to the
custody of Wayne. The latter was not a member of the board of inquiry. Frank
Moore says that, under André's signature to a MS. copy of the "Cow-Chase," some
one wrote :
    " When the epic strain was sung,
    The poet by the neck was hung,
    And to his cost he finds, too late,
    The 'dung-born tribe' decides his fate."

that " Gustavus " was no other than General Arnold. Everything was ripe for the consummation of the plot; both parties were anxious for the end.

It was a gloomy hour in the history of the great struggle,
aside from the contemplated act of foul treason. Charleston
had fallen in May, and an American army there had been
made prisoners. Gates had been defeated near Camden in
August, and another American army dispersed. The South
was in possession of the enemy; New Jersey was in nearly
the same condition, and on Manhattan Island lay a strong
army of veteran British soldiers. This was the moment
sagaciously chosen by Arnold to strike a fatal blow at the
liberties of his country.

At the close of August Arnold wrote to André, in the
usual disguise of commercial phrases, demanding a personal
interview at an American outpost in Westchester County,
the latter to come in the disguise of " John Anderson," a
bearer of intelligence from New York. But André was not
disposed to enter the American lines in disguise. A meeting
of André and Beverly Robinson with General Arnold, at
Dobb's Ferry, on the neutral ground, on September 11th,
was arranged ; but the interview was prevented by provi-
dential interposition—an interposition in favor of the American cause so conspicuously manifested in every stage of this
conspiracy.

Washington had made arrangements for a conference, at
Hartford, on the 20th of September, with the Count de Rochambeau, the commander of the French forces, then at
Newport, Rhode Island, who had come to assist the Americans in their struggle. It was arranged between Arnold and
André that the surrender of West Point should take place
during Washington's absence. A personal interview for the

purpose of settling everything concerning the great transaction was absolutely necessary, and a meeting of the complotters was appointed to take place on the night of the 21st of September, on the west side of the Hudson, in a lonely spot not far from the hamlet of Haverstraw.

Beverly Robinson and a few others were sharers in the great secret; and there were vague rumors in the air that Major André was engaged in an enterprise which, if successful, would end the war, and redound to his honor and secure him great renown—a baronetcy and a brigadiership, perhaps. It is said that Sir Henry Clinton promised these rewards to his adjutant-general. In confirmation of the truth of this assertion, an incident that occurred on the day when André left New York to meet Arnold may here be cited.

On the 20th of September (1780) Colonel Williams, whose headquarters were in the Kip mansion, at Kip's Bay, foot of (present) Thirty-fourth Street, East River, gave a dinner-party to General Sir Henry Clinton and his staff. It was a beautiful, sunny day, and there were exuberant Tories around the banquet-table on that occasion. The spirits of Sir Henry were specially buoyant, for he was anticipating a great victory in the near-future. His accomplished adjutant-general, Major André, was with him.

When the band had ceased playing the favorite dinner air, " The Roast Beef of Old England," many toasts were drunk. At length Colonel Williams arose and said : " Sir Henry, our adjutant-general appears very dull this afternoon. We all know what a brave soldier, what a genial companion, what a charming song-bird he is ; and yet music is, perhaps, the least among his accomplishments. I call upon the adjutant-general for a song." Colonel Williams then said, " Gentlemen, I offer the toast, ' Major John André, our worthy adjutant-general, the brave soldier and accomplished gentleman.' "

The toast was greeted with great applause. Then André arose and said : " Yes, Colonel Williams, I do feel rather serious this afternoon, and I can give no particular reason for it. I will sing, however, as you request me to." Then he sang, with great sweetness and much pathos, the old familiar camp-song, beginning—

> " Why, soldiers, why,
> Should we be melancholy, boys ?
> Why, soldiers, why,
> Whose business 'tis to die !
> For should next campaign
> Send us to Him who made us, boys,
> We're free from pain ;
> But should we remain,
> A bottle and kind landlady
> Makes all well again."

With a trembling and husky voice the usually gay young soldier thanked the company for the honor they had done him, when Sir Henry said : " A word in addition, gentlemen, if you please. The major leaves the city on duty to-night, which will most likely terminate in makir ʒ plain John André *Sir* John André—for success must crown his efforts."

Major André left the hilarious company with a countenance saddened by an indefinable presentiment of impending disaster, and departed on that fatal mission involved in his complot with General Arnold.

André went up the Hudson that evening in the sloop-of-war *Vulture*, twenty-four, to have the arranged personal interview with Arnold. He was accompanied by Beverly Robinson. The vessel was anchored between Teller's (now Croton) Point and Verplanck's Point, and lay there all the

next day. Arnold had agreed to send a boat to the *Vulture*
to convey André to the shore at the appointed time. For
that service he had employed Joshua H. Smith, an intimate
acquaintance and a gentleman farmer, at whose house Mrs.
Arnold had been entertained a few days before, while on her
way to join her husband at his headquarters. Smith's house
is yet standing, upon an eminence known as Treason Hill,
between Stony Point and Haverstraw. It overlooks a picturesque region, with Haverstraw Bay in the foreground.

THE SMITH HOUSE.

The place appointed for the meeting of the conspirators
was at a lonely spot in a thicket at the foot of Torn Mountain, near the west shore of the Hudson, about two miles
below Haverstraw. It was outside the American lines.
Smith appeared in a small boat, with two stout oarsmen,
at the side of the *Vulture* at midnight. André was ready to
accompany him. He covered his scarlet uniform with a

long blue surtout. Clinton had instructed him to have nothing to do with papers of any kind, and he went ashore empty-handed.

It was a little past midnight when André was landed on the beach at the mouth of a little creek. He was conducted by Smith to Arnold's place of concealment, and there in the dimmed starlight these notable conspirators, who had long communed through mysterious epistles, met face to face for the first time. At Arnold's request, Smith went back to his boat to await the return of André, who was to be conveyed again to the *Vulture* before daybreak.

The interview was long protracted. It was not ended when the eastern horizon began to kindle with the dawn. Both men were anxious to complete the business at that time. Arnold had two horses with him, one of them ridden by his servant. He now proposed that André should mount his servant's horse and ride with him to Smith's house and there complete the arrangement. The major reluctantly consented to do so, with the understanding that he was to be conveyed to the *Vulture* as soon as possible.

As the two horsemen approached the little hamlet of Haverstraw they were challenged by a sentinel. André was alarmed. He was, unwittingly, within the American lines; but he had gone too far, however, to recede, and they rode on together to Smith's house. By ten o'clock they had finished their business, when Arnold, after handing André some papers containing all needed information concerning the post to be surrendered, departed in his barge for West Point.

It had been arranged that Sir Henry Clinton should ascend the Hudson with a strong force on the 25th, and attack the important post; and Arnold, after making a show

7

of resistance, should surrender it, with all the men and munitions of war, on the plea of the weakness of the garrison. A
part of the plan was the seizure of Washington, who was to
return on the 27th. For this service the traitor was to receive from the king the commission of brigadier-general in
the royal army, and fifty thousand dollars in gold. The surrender was not effected, but Arnold received the commission, and nearly forty thousand dollars in gold.

When the conspirators arrived at Smith's house at sunrise, André was alarmed at the disappearance of the *Vulture*.
She had been cannonaded from Verplanck's Point, and compelled to drop down the river.

Just after the departure of Arnold, the *Vulture* reap-
peared at her anchorage of the night before. André urged
Smith to take him to the sloop immediately, but he declined,
giving various reasons for his conduct. He was really afraid
to perform the service, and the British adjutant-general was
kept in a state of great anxiety on Treason Hill until evening. Arnold had intimated that the major might be compelled to cross the river and return to New York by land.
To provide for any contingency, he furnished passports, one
to secure to André a safeguard through the American posts
to the neutral ground, and another to secure such safety in
passing down the river in a boat to Dobb's Ferry.

Smith decided that André must return by land. He
tried to procure an American uniform for the major's disguise, but could not, and his guest was compelled to accept
an old purple or crimson coat, trimmed with threadbare
gold lace, and a tarnished beaver hat belonging to Smith.
The rest of his suit was his military undress, nankeen small-
clothes, and white-topped boots. His long surtout with
a cape covered all.

In violation of Clinton's positive orders, André took away the papers which Arnold had given him. These he concealed in his stockings beneath his feet. So equipped, and bearing Arnold's passports, André mounted a black horse which the American general had provided for his use, and at twilight, accompanied by Smith and his negro servant, he crossed the river at the King's Ferry, went safely through the American works at Verplanck's Point, and reluctantly spent the night at a farm-house below the Croton River, within the American lines. The travelers slept together. It was a weary and restless night for André. They arose early and rode on some distance together. After breakfast they parted company at Pine's bridge, André pushing on within the neutral ground. He was induced to leave the road leading to the White Plains, which he had been directed to take, and, turning westward at Chappaqua, he followed another road nearer the river, which led him to Tarrytown. This was a fatal mistake.

The neutral ground, extending from King's Bridge nearly to the Croton River, was swarming with Tories. It was the region of great manors, whose owners were loyalists, and their retainers were their political followers. It was a most uncomfortable dwelling-place for the comparatively few Whig inhabitants. It was infested with gangs of marauders, who were called "cow-boys." They were constantly stealing the cattle of the Whigs and driving them off to the British army in New York. The patriotic inhabitants, especially the young men, armed themselves in defense of their property.

On the morning of Friday, the 23d of September (1780), seven young men, farmers and neighbors—John Paulding, Isaac Van Wart, David Williams, John Yerks and three others—were out on a scout together. They seem to have been a sort of guerrillas, acting independently in intercepting marauders and arresting suspicious-looking travelers. Paulding had been a prisoner in New York a short time before, and had escaped in the disguise of a Hessian coat which a friend had procured for him. This coat he now wore.

Three of the four young men above named were playing cards in a thicket near the highway, half a mile from Tarrytown, at about nine o'clock in the morning, when a well-dressed horseman approached on a black steed. He was a stranger, and the young men concluded to stop him and inquire about his errand. Paulding, who was the leader of the little band, stepped out of the bushes with his musket, and ordered the traveler to halt and give an account of himself. Seeing Paulding with a British military coat on, and knowing that he was far below the American lines and nearer those of the British, the horseman said to the three young scouts:

" My lads, I hope you belong to our party."

" What party ? " asked Paulding.

" The lower party—the British."

" We do," said Paulding.

Completely thrown off his guard, the traveler exclaimed with much animation : " Thank God, I am once more among friends! I am a British officer, out in the country on particular business, and hope you will not detain me a minute."

" We are Americans," said Paulding, seizing the bridle of the horse, "and you are our prisoner."

The traveler was shocked, but, assuming composure, he said, " I must do anything to get along," and with apparent unconcern he pulled from his pocket Arnold's passport, which read :

      " HEADQUARTERS, ROBINSON'S HOUSE, *September 22, 1780.*

"Permit Mr. John Anderson to pass the guards to the White Plains, or below if he chooses, he being on public business by my direction.

          " B. ARNOLD, *Major-General."*

ARNOLD'S PASSPORT.

The suspicions of the young men were now thoroughly aroused. Making the traveler dismount, they searched every part of his clothing, but found nothing of importance.

"Try his boots," said Van Wart.

They compelled him to sit upon a log by the road-side, and, pulling off his boots, they discovered, by the bagging of his stocking-feet, several papers. These Paulding, the only one of the young men who could read, glanced over and exclaimed: ·

" My God ! he is a spy ! "

Major John André, adjutant-general of the British army, was their prisoner, but they did not know it. They believed that he was a British officer, as he himself at first announced. They questioned him closely about the papers in his boots, but he became very reticent. He offered them large bribes to induce them to let him pass. He offered them his gold watch. They refused. " I will give you a hundred guineas and any amount of dry goods," he said. They refused. " I will give you a thousand guineas," he said, "and you can hold me as a hostage till one of your number return with the money."

" We would not let you go for ten thousand guineas ! " said Paulding, in a loud voice. That decision settled the fate of André.

The prisoner then requested his captors to take him to the nearest American post, and ask him no more questions. They complied. He was seated on his horse, which one of them alternately led, while the others marched alongside as guards.

Such was the story of André's capture, as related by the three young men. Major André declared that the sole object of the captors in arresting him was evidently plunder ; that they searched every part of him, even his saddle and his boots, for gold ; and that, if he had possessed sufficient in specie (he had only some Continental bills), he might have easily persuaded them to let him go. But the preponderance of contemporary testimony is in favor of the captors' story. Washington wrote to Congress :

" Their conduct merits our warmest esteem, and I beg leave to add that I think the public would do well to grant them a handsome gratuity. They have prevented, in all probability, our suffering one of the severest strokes that could have been meditated against us."

Congress complimented the captors on their fidelity and patriotism by a resolution of thanks, ordered that an annuity of two hundred dollars in specie should be paid to each out of the public treasury, and directed the Board of War to

(From a Miniature in possession of the late James K. Paulding.)

have a silver medal of appropriate design struck and given to each. These medals Washington presented to the captors in person. Tradition tells us that André would undoubtedly have been released but for the strong will and patriotic impulses of John Paulding, then only twenty-two years of age.

André was delivered to Lieutenant-Colonel Jameson, then in command of Sheldon's dragoons and a few Connecticut militia at North Salem. That honest officer believed the captive to be what Arnold's passport proclaimed him, simply " John Anderson," on public business by direction of his general, and treated him very kindly as such. The prisoner requested Jameson to inform Arnold that John Anderson was a captive, in his custody. The honest, unsuspicious Jameson complied. He wrote to Arnold to this effect, explaining how Anderson came to be a prisoner, and concluded that the simplest way in the matter would be to send the captive to Arnold with the letter! He detailed Lieutenant Allen and four of the militia to take both to headquarters, and at the same time sent the papers found in André's boot by express to Washington, who was then on his way from Hartford.

André was delighted by the turn affairs had taken, for now there appeared a way of escape for both Arnold and himself. The escort with the prisoner were some distance on their way, when Major Benjamin Tallmadge, a vigilant and active officer of the dragoons, returned to Jameson's quarters after a brief absence. Learning all about the capture and the nature of the papers found on the prisoner, he at once pronounced him a spy and Arnold a traitor. He persuaded Jameson to order the return of the prisoner, agreeing to bear all blame himself for the act. The captive was brought back, but, unfortunately, Allen proceeded alone with Jameson's letter to Arnold.

André was committed to the care of Lieutenant King, of

the dragoons, who was convinced, by the prisoner's manner
and other tokens, that he was no ordinary man. Finally, the
captive requested King to walk with him in a large yard
attached to the house in which they were, when the prisoner said, " I must make a confidant of somebody, and I
know not a more proper person than yourself, you have
treated me so kindly." He then made a full confession of
his rank, and gave a brief narrative of his career in America
since his capture at St. Johns. Procuring writing materials,
he wrote the following letter to Washington :

"SALEM, *the 24th September, 1780.*

" SIR: What I have as yet said concerning myself was in
the justifiable attempt to be extricated. I am too little accus-
tomed to duplicity to have succeeded.

" I beg your Excellency will be persuaded that no alter-
ation in the temper of my mind, or apprehension for my safety, induces me to take the step of addressing you, but that it
is to rescue myself from an imputation of having assumed a
mean character for treacherous purposes or self-interest, a
conduct incompatible with the principles which actuate me,
as well as my condition in life. It is to vindicate my fame
that I speak, and not to solicit security. The person in your
possession is Major John André, adjutant-general in the British army.

" The influence of one commander with another in the
army of his adversary is an advantage taken in war. A correspondence for this purpose I held, as confidential, in the
present instance, with his Excellency Sir Henry Clinton.

" To favor it, I agreed to meet upon ground not within
the posts of either army a person who was to give me intelligence. I came up in the *Vulture* man-of-war for this effect,

and was fetched by a boat from the shore to the beach ; being there, I was told that the approach of day would prevent
my return, and that I must be concealed until the next night.
I was in my regimentals, and had fairly risked my person.

"Against my stipulation and without my knowledge be-
forehand, I was conducted within one of your posts. Your
Excellency will conceive my sensation on this occasion, and
will imagine how much more I must have been affected, by
a refusal to reconduct me back the next night as I had been
brought. Thus become a prisoner, I had to concert my
escape. I quitted my uniform, and was passed another way
in the night, without the American posts to neutral ground,
and informed I was beyond all armed parties, and left to
press for New York. I was taken at Tarrytown by some
volunteers. Thus, as I have had the honor to relate, was I
betrayed (being adjutant-general of the British army) into
the vile condition of an enemy in disguise within your posts.

"Having avowed myself a British officer, I have nothing
to reveal but what relates to myself, which is true, on the
honor of an officer and a gentleman. The request I have to
make to your Excellency, and I am conscious I address myself
well, that in any rigor feeling may dictate, a decency of conduct toward me may mark, that, though unfortunate, I am
branded with nothing dishonorable, as no motive could be
mine but the service of my King, and as I was an involuntary
impostor.

"Another request is, that I may be permitted to write
an open letter to Sir Henry Clinton, and another to a friend
for clothes and linen.

"I take the liberty to mention the condition of some
gentlemen at Charlestown, who, being either on parole or
under protection, were engaged in a conspiracy against us.

Though their situation is not exactly similar, they are objects who may be set in exchange for me, or are persons whom the treatment I receive may affect.

" It is no less, sir, in a confidence in the generosity of your mind, than on account of your superior station, that I have chosen to importune you with this letter.

" I have the honor to be, with great respect, sir, your Excellency's most obedient and most humble servant,

" JOHN ANDRÉ, *Adjutant-General.*

" His Excellency General WASHINGTON."

CHAPTER VI.

WASHINGTON lodged at Fishkill, eighteen miles from West Point, on the night of September 24th, and early the next morning (the day appointed for Clinton to ascend the river and receive the surrender of the post in the Highlands) he and his companions reached the vicinity of Arnold's quarters, where they intended to breakfast. He and two or three officers turned aside to inspect a redoubt, while Lafayette, Hamilton, and other young officers, rode forward with a message from their chief to Mrs. Arnold, bidding her not to delay breakfast on his account.

While these officers were at table with Arnold and his wife, a courier arrived with a letter to the general. It was Jameson's letter, brought by Allen, telling Arnold of the arrest of " John Anderson," and the sending of the papers found in his boots to Washington. Arnold glanced at the letter, sat a few minutes in general conversation, and then asked to be excused. His wife perceived anxiety in his countenance, and, leaving the table, followed him out of the room. He commanded Allen not to mention that he had brought a letter from Jameson ; ordered a horse to be saddled and brought to the door immediately, and ascending to his wife's chamber, to which she had retired, he told her in a few hurried words of his perilous situation, and that his life depended upon his instant flight and reaching the British lines in safety.

This awful message smote the young wife and mother fearfully. She screamed and fell at his feet in a swoon. He had not a moment to lose. Leaving her in the care of her maid, he kissed their sleeping babe and hurried to the breakfast-room. Telling the guests that his wife had been taken ill suddenly, and that he was called in haste over to West Point and would return presently, he mounted the horse at the door, dashed down the bridle-path to the river half a mile distant, snatched his pistols from the holsters as he dismounted, and, summoning the crew of his barge, he entered it and ordered them to pull into the middle of the stream and row swiftly down the river, for he bore a flag to the *Vulture*, and must return soon to meet General Washington.

Arnold sat in the prow of his barge. When they came in sight of the *Vulture* he raised a white handkerchief upon a walking-stick. They soon reached the vessel. Arnold ascended to her deck, where he met Colonel Robinson, and briefly related to him the unhappy state of affairs. He tried, in vain, to lure the crew of his barge into the king's service. " If General Arnold likes the King of England, let him serve him ; *we* love our country, and mean to live or die in support of her cause," indignantly exclaimed James Larvey, the coxswain. " So will we," said his companions. They were sent on shore at Teller's Point by the same flag. Arnold sent a letter to Washington, covering one to his wife. He assured the commander-in-chief that his wife was innocent of all knowledge of his act, and entreated him to extend his protection to her and her child. He also exonerated his military family from all participation in his designs.

By the same flag Colonel Robinson wrote to Washington, asserting that, under the circumstances which led to André's arrest, he could not detain him without "the greatest violation of flags and contrary to the usage of all nations"; and, assuming that the American commander would see the matter in the same light, he desired that he would order Major André to be "set at liberty, and allowed to return immediately."

The *Vulture* returned to New York the same evening, and early the next morning Arnold conveyed to General

THE ROBINSON HOUSE.—(From a Sketch by the Author in 1849.)

Clinton the first intelligence of the capture of Major André. Let us go back to Arnold's quarters at Robinson's house, in the Highlands.

Washington arrived, at Arnold's quarters an hour after

the traitor's flight. Informed of the illness of Mrs. Arnold, and that her husband had gone over to West Point, the chief took a hurried breakfast and proceeded thither with all his staff, excepting Colonel Hamilton. As they touched the west shore of the river they were surprised at not re- ceiving the usual cannon-salute.

" Is not General Arnold here?" Washington asked Colo- nel Lamb.

" No, sir," Lamb replied ; " he has not been here for two days, nor have I heard from him in that time."

Meanwhile Hamilton, as Washington's private secretary, had received and examined the papers taken from André's stocking ; also the letters of Jameson, and that of the pris- oner to Washington revealing the conspiracy. Hamilton immediately sought his chief. He met him on his way up from the river, and told him of his discovery of Arnold's treason and of his flight to the *Vulture*. Men were dis- patched to Verplanck's Point to intercept him, but they arrived too late. An order was sent to Colonel Jameson to forward André to West Point immediately. He said to Lafayette and Knox, sadly :

" Arnold is a traitor ! Whom can we trust now?" The whole plot was revealed, and the danger impending over the post was made manifest.

Yet Washington gave no outward sign of excitement. He sent couriers in all directions with orders for the strength- ening of every redoubt, and ordered Greene to put the army at Tappaan in readiness to move toward West Point at a moment's warning. But it was soon evident that the danger was overpast. Informed of Mrs. Arnold's sad condition, he said to one of his aides, " Go to her and inform her that, though my duty required that no means should be neglected to arrest General Arnold, I have great pleasure in acquainting *her* that he is now safe on board a British vessel of war." *¹⁾*

André was brought to the Robinson house early on the 26th (September, 1780). He had been aroused from slumber at midnight to begin a dreary journey in a falling rain, under a strong escort led by Lieutenant King. On the way they were joined by Major Tallmadge and one or two other officers. Tallmadge was made the special custodian of the prisoner from that time until his execution ; and on the evening of the 26th André was conveyed to West Point.

General Greene was in chief command of the American army during Washington's absence. Its headquarters were at Tappaan (usually called Orangetown), a short distance from the west shore of the Hudson. Washington sent secret orders to Greene to receive the prisoner.

" THE '76 STONE HOUSE."

On the morning of the 28th André, with a strong escort, went down the river in a barge, landed at the King's Ferry, and journeyed to Tappaan on horseback. There he was lodged in a substantial stone dwelling belonging to Mr.

Maybie, known, in our day, as a tavern, by the name of
" The '76 Stone House."

On this journey of a day, Tallmadge and André, who were
about equal in age, had much free conversation. The prisoner's custodian, like every one else, was fascinated by the
young soldier, and was deeply impressed with sympathy for
him. In reply to a question by Tallmadge, André said that,
in the enterprise in which he was engaged, all he sought was
*military glory, the applause of his king and his country, and per-
haps a brigadiership.* He asked Tallmadge in what light he
would be regarded by General Washington and a military
tribunal. Tallmadge tried to evade an answer, but, being
pressed, he said :

" I had a much-loved classmate in Yale College by the
name of Nathan Hale, who entered the army in 1775. Immediately after the battle of Long Island, General Washington wanted information respecting the strength, position,
and probable movements of the enemy. Captain Hale ten-
dered his services, went over to Brooklyn, and was taken
just as he was passing the outposts of the enemy on his
return. *Do you remember the sequel of the story ?* " " Yes,"
said André, " he was hanged as a spy. But you surely do
not consider his case and mine alike." " Yes, precisely
similar ; and similar will be your fate," said Tallmadge.

In general orders on the 26th Greene proclaimed, " Treason of the blackest dye was discovered yesterday." He then
gave a general account of the affair to the army and the people. It created wide-spread indignation and alarm, but the
latter feeling was tempered by the concluding words of the
order: " Arnold has made his escape to the enemy ; but Major André, the adjutant-general of the British army, who
came out as a spy to negotiate the business, is our prisoner."

The news of the capture of André, and this ominous general order, produced intense excitement in both armies, and especially within the British lines. The evident sympathy of Washington and some of his officers for the prisoner when he was brought to Tappaan, created much feeling in the American army. Some of the officers declared that if they were not to be protected against such treacherous conduct, and this spy be pardoned, it was time to leave the army. In a manuscript account of the affair now before me, written by Elias Boudinot, LL. D., the eminent American commissary of prisoners, he observed :

" Though these were their sentiments, they were only murmured from tent to tent. A few days convinced them that they had a commander-in-chief who knew how to make his compassion for the unfortunate and his duty to those who depended upon him for protection to harmonize and influence his conduct. He treated Major André with the greatest tenderness, while he carried the sentence of the council into execution according to the laws of war. At New York, when the first account of André's capture and condemnation arrived, the officers and citizens laughed at the idea that the ' rebels ' would dare to execute the adjutant-general of the British army ; but, if it should take place, vengeance in every form should be taken sevenfold. But, when it was known that André was no more, General Clinton shut himself up for three days, and every one at the Coffee-House and other public places hung their heads, and scarcely an observation relative to it escaped their lips."

Washington had returned to his headquarters at Tappaan,* and ordered a meeting of a board of officers on the

---

* This building is yet standing, and is in nearly the same condition as it was in 1780, at which time it belonged to John de Windt, a native of the Island of St.

8

29th, to make careful inquiries and report their opinion "of the light in which he [the prisoner] ought to be considered, and what punishment ought to be inflicted." The board consisted of six major-generals and eight brigadier-generals. The court of inquiry was held in the Dutch church at

WASHINGTON'S HEADQUARTERS AT TAPPAAN.

Tappaan. General Greene presided. When André was brought before his judges, he gave a detailed statement of the facts, and did not deny any of the specifications presented by the judge-advocate, John Laurance. After careful deliberation the board reported that the prisoner "ought to be considered as a spy from the enemy, and that, agreeably to the law and usages of nations, it is their opinion he ought to suffer death." "André met the result," wrote Colonel Ham-

Thomas. By a peculiar arrangement of bricks in its front wall, the date of its construction—1700—may be seen. In a large room which Washington occupied as his office, and where André's death-warrant was signed, the spacious fireplace was surrounded by Dutch pictorial tiles, when I visited and made the above sketch, in 1849.

ilton, "with manly firmness. 'I foresee my fate,' he said, 'and though I pretend not to play the hero, or be indifferent to life, yet I am reconciled to whatever may happen, conscious that misfortune, not guilt, has brought it upon me.'"

Washington approved the finding of the court of inquiry, and sentenced André to be hung as a spy on the first day of October, at five o'clock in the afternoon. He sent an account of the proceedings of the court and a letter from André to Sir Henry Clinton.*

Meanwhile great exertions had been made to save André from his sad fate. General Clinton wrote to Washington (September 26th) that André was not a legal spy, for a flag of truce had been sent to receive him, and passports were granted for his return. On receiving the papers from Washington, Sir Henry wrote a second letter to the American chief commander, expressing the opinion that the board "had not been rightly informed of all the circumstances," and asked a postponement of the execution until a conference might be held. The request was granted. The execution was postponed one day. General Greene met General Robertson and others at Dobb's Ferry, not as an officer, but as a private gentleman, but nothing occurred to warrant a change in the opinion of the board of inquiry and the decision of Washington.†

---

* This letter evinced great tenderness of feeling toward his commander. He declared that the events connected with his coming within the American lines were contrary to his own intentions, and avowed the object of his letter to be to remove from Sir Henry's mind any suspicion that he (André) imagined he was bound by his Excellency's orders to expose himself to what had happened.

† General Robertson bore a letter from Arnold to Washington, which he reserved until all oral arguments had failed, when he read it to the gentlemen of the conference. Had there been a chance for coming to an understanding in regard to André before, this impudent letter from the traitor would have destroyed it. Arnold said : " If, after this just and candid opinion of Major André's case, the

The Americans would gladly have saved the life of André could Arnold have been given up to them. Efforts to
that end were made. Unofficial overtures were made to
Clinton to exchange Arnold for André, but honor forbade
the act. All efforts in this direction failed.

On the morning of October 1st, the day on which André
expected to die, he wrote the following touching note to
Washington:

"SIR: ·Buoyed above the terror of death by the consciousness of a life devoted to honorable pursuits, and
stained with no action that can give remorse, I trust that the
request I make to your Excellency at this serious period, and
which is to soften my last moments, will not be rejected.

"Sympathy toward a soldier will surely induce your
Excellency and a military tribunal to adapt the mode of my
death to the feelings of a man of honor.

"Let me hope, sir, that if aught in my character im-
presses you with esteem toward me, if aught in my misfortune marks me as the victim of policy and not of resentment, I shall experience the operation of those feelings in
your breast by being informed that I am not to die on a
gibbet.

" I have the honor to be your Excellency's most obedient
and most humble servant,   JOHN ANDRÉ."

Colonel Hamilton urged Washington to comply with
André's request, but the commander could not grant it.

---

board of general officers adhere to their former opinion, I shall suppose it dictated
by passion and resentment ; and, if that gentleman should suffer the severity of the
sentence, I shall think myself bound by every tie of duty and honor to retaliate on
such unhappy persons of your army as may fall in my power, that the respect due
to flags and the law of nations may be better understood and observed."

Unwilling to wound the feelings of the prisoner by a refusal, he did not reply to the note.

On the preceding evening André wrote letters to his
mother, sisters, Miss Seward, and other friends, and made a
pen-and-ink sketch of himself sitting at a table with a pen
in his hand. On the following morning he made a rude
sketch, with pen and ink, depicting the scene of his passage
from the *Vulture* to the shore, when he went to meet Arnold.*

At noon on the 2d day of October, 1780, Major André
was executed upon an eminence near Tappaan village, in the
presence of a vast concourse of people. He was dressed in
full military costume and white top-boots. He was taken
to the gallows—a cross-piece between two moderate-sized
trees—by a procession of nearly all the field-officers, excepting Washington and his staff, who remained at headquarters. General Greene led the cavalcade, which passed between two files of soldiers, extending from the prison up to
the fatal spot. The prisoner's step was firm, and he did not
falter until he saw the gallows, and knew he was to be
hanged as a felon and not shot as a soldier. His hesitation
was only for a moment.

A baggage-wagon, bearing a plain pine coffin, had been
driven under the gallows. A grave had been dug near by.
Into the wagon the prisoner stepped and, taking the rope
from the hangman, adjusted it to his neck, and tied a white
handkerchief over his eyes. Then Adjutant-General Scam-

---

* The size of the original drawing from which the above sketch was made is
twelve by seven inches. It will be observed that André has but one oarsman, instead of two, as was the case. The drawing was found on his table by his servant
after the execution, and delivered by him at New York to Lieutenant-Colonel
Crosby of André's regiment (the Twenty-second), and who, on his return to England, caused a *fac-simile* of it to be produced by the mezzotint process of engraving.

mell read the order for the execution in a clear voice, and at its conclusion told André that he might speak if he desired it. The prisoner lifted the handkerchief from his eyes and, bowing courteously to General Greene and his officers, said in firm voice, "All I request of you, gentle-men, is that, while I acknowledge the propriety of my sentence, you will bear me witness that I die like a brave man." In an undertone he murmured, "It will be but a momentary pang." The wagon was driven swiftly from under him, and in a few minutes he ceased to exist.

"Thus died in the bloom of life," wrote Dr. Thacher, a surgeon of the Continental army, who was present, "the accomplished Major André, the pride of the royal army and the valued friend of Sir Henry Clinton." The same authority wrote that André's regimentals, which had been brought up to Tappaan by his servant, were handed to that servant, and he was buried near one of the trees which formed the gibbet.

CHAPTER VII.

ALMOST universal sympathy was felt and expressed for Major André. He was undoubtedly an involuntary spy. The court of inquiry which decided his fate came to their conclusions with regret; but duty, the law of nations, and the exigencies of war, compelled them to give such a verdict as they did. Washington signed his death-warrant with reluctance and with much emotion. All the American officers were moved by deep sympathy for him. Some of the younger officers—Lafayette, Hamilton, Tallmadge, and others—were enamored with him, and became attached to him.

"From the few days of intimate intercourse I had with him," wrote Tallmadge, "I became so deeply attached to Major André that I could remember no instance when my affections were so fully absorbed by any man." The multitude who saw the execution were deeply moved with compassion. Dr. Thacher says the tears of thousands fell on that occasion. The event made a deep impression upon both armies. The king specially honored the memory of André by ordering a notable mural monument to be erected in Westminster Abbey, near the " Poets' Corner." A picture of this monument is seen in the engraving.* The memorial was executed in statuary marble, and is about seven and a half feet in height. It represents a sarcophagus with a device in low relief, and elevated upon a paneled pedestal, upon which are appropriate inscriptions.† On the sarcophagus is a representation of Washington and his officers in his tent at the moment when he received the report of the court of inquiry ; at the same time a messenger has arrived

---

* The original drawing from which the engraving was made was received from London in 1849 by the author of this little work, together with a copy of a profile likeness of André—simply the head and shoulders—said to have been drawn by himself.

† Upon a panel is the following inscription : " Sacred to the memory of Major JOHN ANDRÉ, who, raised to the rank of Adjutant-General of the British Army in America, and employed in an important and hazardous enterprise, fell a sacrifice to his zeal for his king and country, on the 2d of October, A. D. 1780, eminently beloved and esteemed by the army in which he served, and lamented even by his foes. His gracious sovereign, KING GEORGE THE THIRD, has caused this monument to be erected."

After the removal of André's remains to Westminster Abbey, as mentioned in the text, the following inscription was cut upon the base of the pedestal :

" The remains of Major JOHN ANDRÉ were, on the 10th of August, 1821, removed from Tappaan by JAMES BUCHANAN, Esq., his Majesty's Consul at New York, under instructions from his Royal Highness the DUKE OF YORK, and, with the permission of the Dean and Chapter, finally deposited in a grave contiguous to this monument on the 28th of November, 1821."

with the letter of André to Washington asking for a soldier's death. On the right is a guard of Continental soldiers, and a tree on which André was executed. Two men are pre-

ANDRÉ'S MONUMENT IN WESTMINSTER ABBEY.

paring the prisoner for execution, while at the foot of the tree sit Mercy and Innocence. On the top of the sarcophagus is the British lion, and the figure of Britannia, who is lamenting the fate of André. The king settled a pension upon the family of André, and, to wipe out the imputed stain produced by his death as a spy, the honor of knight-hood was conferred upon his brother. ✍

As related in the inscription on the pedestal of André's monument, given in a foot-note, Mr. Buchanan caused his re-mains to be disinterred and sent to England. Two small cedar-trees were growing near the grave wherein lay his remains. A portion of one of these was sent with the re-mains, and, at the suggestion of the consul, the duke caused a snuff-box to be made of it for the Rev. Mr. Demorest, of Tappaan, who gave Mr. Buchanan much assistance in his undertaking. It was elegant in design, was lined with gold, and was inscribed with the words :   .

"From his Royal Highness the Duke of York, to mark his sense of the Rev. John Demorest's liberal attention upon the occasion of the removal of the remains of the late Major André, at Tappaan, on the 10th of August, 1821."

The surviving sisters of André sent a silver cup to Mr. Demorest, with a suitable inscription ; also an inkstand to the British consul.

Two monuments have been erected at different times on the spot where André was executed, each with the sole pur-pose of commemorating this very important·event in our national history, and to mark the exact locality of ·its occur-rence. One of these monuments was set up by James Lee,* a public-spirited New York merchant, nearly forty years

---

* It was chiefly through the liberality and personal influence of Mr. Lee that the funds were raised for procuring the fine bronze equestrian statue of WASHING-TON, by H. K. Brown, at Union Square, New York. That was the first statue erected in the open air in that city, and is not surpassed in artistic merit by any since set up there.

ago. It consisted of a small bowlder, upon the upper surface of which were cut the words, " ANDRÉ WAS EXECUTED OCTOBER 2, 1780." It was on the right side of a lane which ran from the highway from Tappaan village to old Tappaan, on the westerly side of a large peach-orchard, and about a mile from Washington's headquarters. I visited the spot in 1849, and made a drawing of this simple memorial-stone for my " Pictorial Field Book of the Revolution." In a footnote of that work (vol. i, p. 772) I said, " A more elegant and durable monument should be erected on the spot."

BOWLDER-MONUMENT.

A "more elegant and durable monument" was placed on the same spot a few years ago by another public-spirited New York merchant, Mr. Cyrus W. Field, and bears an inscription written by the late Rev. Arthur Penrhyn Stanley, the Dean of Westminster. When that eminent divine and earnest friend of our country and admirer of our free institutions was about to visit the United States in 1878, he made a list of the objects and localities which he desired to see while here. Among these was the place of André's execution.

While Dean Stanley was visiting Mr. Field at his country residence on the eastern bank of the Hudson, nearly opposite Tappaan, he with his two traveling companions and their host crossed the river, and, with one or two citizens of Tappaan, visited places of historic interest in the vicinity. They found that nothing marked the place of André's execution, and that it had even been a subject of controversy. The bowlder-monument had been removed several years before. The dean expressed his surprise and regret that no object indicated the locality of such an important historical event, when Mr. Field said he would erect a memorial-stone there at his own expense upon certain conditions. A few days afterward (October, 1878) he wrote to a citizen of Tappaan :

"I am perfectly willing to erect a monument on 'André Hill' [so named by the people in commemoration of the event which occurred there], and the dean will write an inscription, if the people who own the land will make a grant of about twenty square feet for the purpose."

So soon as it became known that Mr. Field proposed to erect a memorial-stone at Tappaan, a correspondent of a New York morning journal denounced the intention, upon the wholly erroneous assumption that it was to be a "monument in honor of Major André, the British spy." Other correspondents, equally uninformed, followed with denunciations. A storm of apparently indignant protests, or worse, ensued ; and one writer, lacking courage to give his name, made a threat that, if Mr. Field should set up a memorial-stone upon the place where André was executed, "ten thousand men" were ready to pull it down and cast it into the river! These writers, many of whom concealed their real names, created considerable feeling in the public mind unfavorable to the project, and elicited a multitude of appeals to the patriotism and the prejudices of the American people, to oppose what?—a phantom!

This intemperate and unwise correspondence continued several weeks. There were calm defenders of Mr. Field's motives in proposing to erect a monument, by persons who were well informed and had a clear perception of the intent and importance of such an act. The discussion was fruitful of some good. It had the salutary effect of calling public attention to the claims of NATHAN HALE, the notable martyr spy of the Revolution, to a memorial tribute—a public recognition of his virtues and his deeds—which had been so long deferred by our people. These claims were now earnestly advocated, not only by Mr. Field's critics, but by patriotic citizens. Considerable sums of money were offered for the laudable purpose of erecting a suitable monument in the city of New York to the memory of Hale. Several persons offered one hundred dollars each.

Before the visit of Mr. Field and the dean, Mr. Henry Whittemore, a public-spirited citizen of Tappan, and Secretary of the Rockland County Historical Society, had found four living men who were present at the disinterment of André's remains in 1821. With these men he went to "André Hill," where they identified the place of the spy's grave.* The requisite plot of ground was secured by Mr.

---

* Mr. Whittemore had procured this identification fully six months before the visit of Mr. Field and his guests, with the view to have a memorial-stone placed upon the spot. He had consulted with the owner of the land about it. The latter believed it would enhance the value of his property, and favored the project.

Field, who was compelled to buy many surrounding acre:
at an exorbitant price. Then, relying upon the good sense
the intelligence, and the patriotism of the American peopl(
for a just appreciation of his motives, he proceeded to hav(
a memorial-stone prepared.

Soon after Dean Stanley returned home he wrote th(
promised inscription, and, in a letter to Mr. Whittemor(
(January, 1879), he said:

" I have sent to Mr. Cyrus W. Field the inscription sug
gested. Perhaps you will kindly see that the facts are cor

DEAN STANLEY'S AUTOGRAPH.

rectly stated. It is desirable that the inscription shoulc
contain neither an attack nor a defense of André, but onl)

an expression of sympathy with him in his tragical fate, and with Washington for the difficult circumstances in which the judges were placed.

" A wreath of autumn leaves from the Hudson I had placed on the monument in the abbey attracts universal attention. I have also the silver medals of Washington's headquarters, and the old Dutch church at Tappaan.

" I remain, yours gratefully,

" A. P. STANLEY." *

On the 2d of October, 1879, the ninety-ninth anniversary of the execution of André, the monument prepared by Mr. Field's order, and placed over the spot where the spy was buried,' was uncovered in the presence of representatives of the Historical Societies of New York, and Rockland County, of officers of the army of the United States, of the newspaper press and other gentlemen, and a few ladies. At noon, the hour of the day when André was executed, Mr. Field directed the workmen to uncover the memorial. There was no pomp or ceremony on the occasion. Not a speech was uttered, nor a token of applause given.

From " André Hill " the company went with Mr. Whittemore to his home in Washington's headquarters and the room in which André's death-warrant was signed. While there the neglect of the memory of Nathan Hale, shown by the American people, was spoken of, when Mr. Field said :

"Gentlemen, if I may be granted permission, I will erect a monument in memory of Nathan Hale on the spot where

---

* Above may be seen a *fac-simile* of the last paragraph of Dean Stanley's letter.

he suffered death in the city of New York, if the place may be found."

Several years ago Mr. Field made a similar offer to the New York Historical Society.* More than thirty years before, he was a contributor to the fund raised to erect the modest monument in memory of Hale at South Coventry, delineated on page 26; and he was next to the largest contributor to the fund for procuring the bronze statue of a captor of André that surmounts the monument at Tarrytown, which commemorates that important event.

The memorial-stone erected at Tappaan is composed of a shaft of Quincy gray granite, standing upon a pedestal of the same material. The whole structure is about nine feet in height from the ground to the apex. It is perfectly chaste in design. There is no ornamentation. The granite is highly polished. It stands upon an elevation, about two miles from the Hudson River, and thirty yards from the boundary-line between New York and New Jersey, and overlooks a beautiful country.† On its west side it bears the following inscription, written by Dean Stanley:

---

* The letter of Mr. Field conveying his generous offer to the New York Historical Society (September, 1880) was referred to the Executive Committee. They warmly recommended its favorable consideration by the society. In their report, referring to the event commemorated by the memorial-stone at Tappaan, the committee said it was an "event which, perhaps, more signally than any other act of his life, illustrates the wisdom and firmness of Washington under circumstances of peculiar trial, in which even his devoted followers were disposed to question his humanity, if not his justice, and almost to fall in with the sentimental calumny of the day, which has been so often reviewed and refuted as to become ridiculous. The memorial-stone of André's execution is a monument to Washington."

† The engraving is from the original drawing of the architect. Just below the inscription, at the bottom of the shaft, is cut "ARTHUR PENRHYN STANLEY, DEAN OF WESTMINSTER."

"HERE DIED, OCTOBER 2, 1780,
MAJOR JOHN ANDRÉ, OF THE BRITISH ARMY,
WHO, ENTERING THE AMERICAN LINES
ON A SECRET MISSION TO BENEDICT ARNOLD,
FOR THE SURRENDER OF WEST POINT,
WAS TAKEN PRISONER, TRIED AND CONDEMNED AS A SPY.
HIS DEATH,
THOUGH ACCORDING TO THE STERN RULE OF WAR,
MOVED EVEN HIS ENEMIES TO PITY;
AND BOTH ARMIES MOURNED THE FATE
OF ONE SO YOUNG AND SO BRAVE.
IN 1821 HIS REMAINS WERE REMOVED TO WESTMINSTER ABBEY.
A HUNDRED YEARS AFTER THE EXECUTION
THIS STONE WAS PLACED ABOVE THE SPOT WHERE HE LAY,
BY A CITIZEN OF THE UNITED STATES, AGAINST WHICH HE FOUGHT,
NOT TO PERPETUATE THE RECORD OF STRIFE,
BUT IN TOKEN OF THOSE BETTER FEELINGS
WHICH HAVE SINCE UNITED TWO NATIONS,
ONE IN RACE, IN LANGUAGE, AND IN RELIGION,
WITH THE HOPE THAT THIS FRIENDLY UNION
WILL NEVER BE BROKEN."

On the north face:

"HE WAS MORE UNFORTUNATE THAN CRIMINAL."
"AN ACCOMPLISHED MAN AND GALLANT OFFICER."
GEORGE WASHINGTON.

The first of these two lines was quoted from a letter of Washington to Count de Rochambeau, October 10, 1780. (See Sparks's " Life and Writings of Washington," vol. vii, p. 241.) The second line is from the sentence of a letter written by Washington to Colonel John Laurens on the 13th of October. (See Sparks, vol. vii, p. 256.)

On the north face of the stone are the words:

"SUNT LACRYMÆ RERUM ET MENTEM MORTALIA TANGUNT."

The east front was left blank for another inscription.

Such, in a few sentences, is the story of the erection of the memorial-stone at Tappaan by Mr. Field. The idea was

9

the product of spontaneous thought, elicited by a special occasion. The sole object to be attained is the laudable and patriotic one of perpetuating, by a visible record, the memory of one of the most important events in our history,

MEMORIAL AT TAPPAAN.

at the place of its occurrence. That event has two prominent aspects, namely: the courage, patriotism, faith in the American people, and the unswerving fidelity in the discharge of a momentous trust, of our beloved Washington and his officers, in the face of most extraordinary temptations to do otherwise; and the execution as a spy of the adjutant-general of the British army, while that army, twenty thousand strong, was lying only a few miles distant, and supported by powerful ships of war.

These were the events to be commemorated by this memorial-stone, and not the name or character of any individual. It was no more a monument "in honor of Major André, the British spy," than was the monument of white marble, twenty-five feet in height, which was erected by patriotic men, in 1853, to mark the spot at Tarrytown where the spy was captured, or the naming of the rivulet near which it stands "André Brook." Surely every intelligent and right-minded American, clearly comprehending the truth of the whole matter, will award to Mr. Field the meed of praise for his generous and patriotic deed.

An attempt was made on the night of November 3, 1885, to destroy the beautiful memorial-stone at Tappaan by an explosion of dynamite. The pedestal was shattered into pieces, but the shaft was only shaken from its perpendicular position. This crime was the logical result of persistent misrepresentation of the character and intent of the memorial in some of the newspapers. Twice before, attempts had been made to destroy it; the first time by a defacement of the inscription by a misguided person who, on a dark night, battered the letters, many of them almost beyond recognition. The destroyer* left a small American flag hanging over the monument from a stick, supported by a pile of stones, upon the apex; also the following lines, the product, evidently, of one moved by a spirit of conscious untruthfulness, or of profound ignorance of the character of the object assailed :

---

* It was ascertained that the perpetrator of the crime was a "crank"—a printer, in the city of New York—who, after eluding the officers of the law for some time, finally died.

" Too long hath stood the traitor's shaft,
    A monument to shame,
Built up to praise the traitor's craft,
    To sanctify ill fame.
Are freemen bound to still forbear,
    And meekly still implore,
When conquered foes their altars rear
    Within our very door .

" This vulgar and insulting stone
    Would honor for all time,
Not sneaking André's death alone,
    But black Ben Arnold's crime.
And they, who thus can glorify
    The traitor and his deeds,
Themselves high treason would employ
    If 'twould fulfill their needs.

" Americans ! resolve, proclaim
    That on our own dear land,
Never, while the people reign,
    Shall treason's statue stand !
And he who dares erect it next,
    On fair Columbia's breast,
With furtive or with false pretext,
    Shall dangle from its crest ! "

The second attempt to destroy the memorial-stone was
made on a dark night. Nitro-glycerine or dynamite was
used for the purpose. The explosion was heard for miles
around. The perpetrator of the deed was not discovered.
The stones of the pedestal were shattered, but the shaft remained in an upright position.

Mr. Field had the damages to the memorial repaired.
He designed to have the acres around it fashioned into a
handsome little park. He also proposed to erect within the
grounds a fire-proof building for the use of the Rockland
County Historical and Forestry Society as a depository of
historical and other relics of that county, the building to be

presented to the society, and the park to the citizens of Tappaan, as a free gift. The outrage of November 3, 1885, may frustrate this generous plan.

Two days after that outrage, a New York morning journal of large circulation and wide influence declared that "the malignity with which the people about Tappaan regard Mr. Field's monument to André appears to be settled and permanent." To this grave indictment of the inhabitants of a portion of Rockland County as participants in the crime, that people responded by resolutions unanimously adopted at an indignation meeting held at the Reformed Church at Tappaan on the evening of the 9th. They denounced the charge as utterly untrue, expressed their belief that no person in the vicinity had "the remotest connection" with the crime; that it was desirable to have the place of André's execution indicated by a memorial-stone with a suitable inscription, and commended Mr. Field for his zeal in perpetuating events of the Revolution in such a manner.*

In the foregoing narrative I have endeavored to present a brief, plain, and truthful story of the memorial at Tappaan, about which so much has been said and written. I have fashioned it from trustworthy materials. I have simply recorded the facts, and leave the readers to form their own conclusions.

✗ The monument at Tarrytown has been alluded to. It was erected in 1853, on the spot where tradition says Major André was captured, to commemorate that event. It bore upon a tablet the following inscription:

" On this spot, the 23d of September, 1780, the spy, Major

---

* A petition addressed to the Governor of the State, asking him to assist in an effort to discover the perpetrator of the crime, was signed by a large number of the most respectable citizens of Rockland County.

MONUMENT AND STATUE AT TARRYTOWN.

John André, Adjutant-General of the British Army, was captured by John Paulding, David Williams, and Isaac Van Wart, all natives of this county. History has told the rest.

"The people of Westchester County have erected this monument as well to commemorate a great event as to testify their high estimation of that integrity and patriotism which, rejecting every temptation, rescued the United States from most imminent peril by baffling the acts of a spy and the plots of a traitor. Dedicated October 7, 1853."

The citizens of Westchester County, desirous of giving more significance to this monument, caused its conical shaft to be removed, and in its place erected a bronze statue of a captor—a young volunteer soldier. This statue is the work of the accomplished sculptor, Mr. O'Donovan, of New York.

The monument and statue were unveiled in the presence of thousands of spectators on the centennial of the event commemorated—the 23d of September, 1880. On that occasion Samuel J. Tilden presided. A prayer was offered by the venerable son of one of the captors, Isaac Van Wart, and an oration was pronounced by Chauncey M. Depew. General James Husted was the marshal of the day.

On one face of the monument is the old inscription, and upon another, next to the highway, is a fine bronze *bas-relief* representing the scene of the capture. This also is from the *atelier* of Mr. O'Donovan. An excellent picture of this work of art and of the statue may be found in the "Memorial Souvenir of the Monument Association," prepared by Dr. Sargent C. Husted, secretary of the association.

MONODY ON MAJOR ANDRÉ.

Anna Seward.

THE AUTHOR OF THE MONODY.

ANNA SEWARD, the abiding friend and ever-faithful correspondent of Major André until his death, was a daughter
of Thomas Seward, the canon-resident of Lichfield Cathedral. She was born at Eyam, in Derbyshire, England, in
1747. Her education, superior to that of most girls of her
time, was superintended by her father, who was a graduate
of Oxford, a man of great moral worth, and noted for his
scholarship.

Miss Seward evinced a taste and a genius for poetic com-
position at a very early age, and before she reached the
period of young womanhood she attracted the attention of
local literary characters. She became a great favorite of
Dr. Samuel Johnson, who was a native of Lichfield and
was a frequent guest at the house of her father. On one
occasion, when she was about fourteen years of age, she
wrote a clever poetical address of welcome to Dr. Johnson,
which greatly pleased the recipient. Miss Seward is often
incidentally mentioned in Boswell's "Life of Johnson."
Writing of a visit at Mr. Seward's in 1775, when Anna was
twenty-eight years of age, Boswell, Johnson's shadow, says,
"And now, for the first time, I had the pleasure of seeing
his celebrated daughter, Miss Anna Seward, to whom I have
since been indebted for many civilities."

Miss Seward's first acquaintance with young André, her

interest in his love-affair with Honora Sneyd, and her pleasant epistolary and personal intercourse with him until his departure for America, have been referred to in the early portions of the brief notice of that young soldier's career contained in this volume. During his service in America she was his constant correspondent; and she first informed him of the death of Honora a short time before his own tragic exit from earth.

The circumstances attending the death of her friend inspired Miss Seward to write her most notable and most admired poem, " Monody on Major André." She was then thirty-three years old. It was printed for the author at Lichfield early in 1781. Being consonant in its utterances with the feelings of the British public at that time, it had a large sale, and produced a powerful sensation. She received congratulatory letters from literary people and others in various parts of the kingdom. No man was more delighted with it than was Dr. Johnson, " the colossus of English literature."

Johnson was a fierce Tory, and hated the Americans with a spirit of savage ferocity. On one occasion, while at Lichfield, he said, " I am willing to love all mankind, excepting an American." He called them " rascals," " robbers and pirates," and angrily exclaimed, " I'd burn and destroy them !" Boswell says Miss Seward, who was present at this outburst of passion, and whose feelings were favorable to the American cause, boldly rebuked Johnson, saying, " Sir, this is an instance that we are most violent against those we have most injured." This delicate but keen reproach irritated Johnson still more, and, says Boswell, " he roared out another tremendous volley, which one might fancy could be heard across the Atlantic." But Johnson and Anna Seward remained good friends until a short time before the death of the former. They corresponded with each other, and frequently met in social circles.

I have said Dr. Johnson was delighted by Miss Seward's "Monody." He exhibited that delight in the most public manner by writing and publishing in the "Gentleman's Magazine," over his own signature, the following poetic epistle to the author:

"TO MISS SEWARD, ON HER MONODY ON MAJOR ANDRÉ:

" Above the frigid etiquette of form,
With the same animated feelings warm,
I come, fair maid, enamored of thy lays,
With tribute verse, to swell the note of praise.
Nor let the gentle Julia's * hand disclaim
The bold intrusion of an honest strain.
Nor is it mine alone—'tis the full voice
Of such as honor with no vulgar choice,†
Of such as feel each glowing line along
Once the bright subject of an humble song.‡
The treasures of the female heart make known
By copying the soft movements of her own.
Woman should walk arrayed in her own robe,
The hope, the boast, the blessing of the globe.
" *Shrewsbury.*   S. JOHNSON."

Miss Seward's "Monody" was dedicated to Sir Henry Clinton. To it were appended three letters written to her by young André immediately after his betrothal to and personal separation from Honora Sneyd. These I have appended to the "Monody." The printed copy of that poem, before me, bears the autograph signature of Anna Seward at the end.

---

* André in his correspondence with Miss Seward on the topic of Honora addressed her as "Julia."

† A reading society at Shrewsbury is here alluded to.

‡ Alluding to an "Essay on Woman," written by Johnson.

It was not long after Johnson's poetical epistle to the author of the " Monody " appeared before an interruption of the goodly feeling between him and his fair friend occurred. In 1782 Johnson's " Lives of the British Poets" appeared, in which he severely criticised the poetry of her cherished friend Thomas Hayley. Ever ready and prompt to defend heroically those she had learned to esteem, she instantly took fire at the attack, and she wrote letters to her friends which were far from complimentary to Johnson. To Hayley she wrote :

" You have seen Dr. Johnson's ' Lives of the Poets.' They have excited your generous indignation. A heart like Hayley's would shrink astonished to perceive a mind so enriched with the power of genius capable of such cool malignity. Yet the ' Gentleman's Magazine ' praised these unworthy efforts to blight the laurels of undoubted fame. Oh, that the venom may fall where it ought ! "

Animadversions by Miss Seward more severe than this found their way, without her consent, into the public prints, and deeply offended Dr. Johnson. The breach thus made was never healed. Miss Seward refused to retract a word, but persisted in her utterances. Sometimes, even after the death of Dr. Johnson, in 1784, they were spiced with attacks upon his personal character. These attacks drew from Boswell a defense of his dead friend, whom he almost adored, and in 1793 he and Miss Seward carried on a spirited controversy in the " Gentleman's Magazine."

Miss Seward's writings in verse and prose were quite voluminous. The latter, consisting of her literary correspondence from 1784 to 1807, was published in six volumes in the latter year. Her poetical works, with extracts from her literary correspondence, edited by Sir Walter Scott, were

published in three volumes in 1810. Next to her " Monody," in point of excellence and popularity, was her " Elegy
on Captain James Cook," the famous circumnavigator of
the globe. Of this performance Sir Walter Scott said, " It
conveyed a high impression of the original power of the
author."

The literary fame of Anna Seward has not been enduring, and she, who was a conspicuous figure in the world of
letters in England during the last quarter of the eighteenth
century, is now almost forgotten. Her known social relations to Major André, and her " Monody," have perpetuated
her memory in the minds of Americans. It is said that,
when she was fully informed of all the circumstances connected with the death of André, she was satisfied that she
had been unjust toward Washington in her animadversions
upon his character in her poem, and expressed a regret that
she had so misjudged him.

Miss Seward, in a letter to her friend Miss Ponsonby, related that several years after the peace a friend of Washington's, an American officer, introduced himself to her (Miss
Seward), saying he was commissioned by General Washington to call upon her and assure her that no circumstance
of his life had been so mortifying as to be censured in the
" Monody " on André as the pitiless author of his ignominious fate ; that he had labored to save him ; and that he requested his friend to leave with Miss Seward a package of
papers which he had sent, consisting of copies of the records
of the court-martial, etc. " The American officer referred
to," says Sargent, " is supposed to have been Colonel Hum-
phreys."

Various opinions have been expressed concerning the
writings of Miss Seward. The literary circle of Lichfield,

of which she was the central figure, appears to have been a mutual-admiration society. The productions of each member appear to have been eulogized by every other member. Her friend, the celebrated Dr. Erasmus Darwin, declared that she was "the inventress of epic elegy"; the eccentric philosopher Day called her a "prodigy of genius"; while the wits of London gently ridiculed the pretensions of the literary Lichfieldians. Horace Walpole wrote: "Misses Seward and Williams, and a half a dozen more of these harmonious virgins, have no imagination, no novelty. Their thoughts and phrases are like their gowns—old remnants cut and turned." The Rev. Alexander Dyce wrote: "She was endowed with considerable genius, and with an ample portion of that fine enthusiasm which sometimes may be taken for it; but her taste was far from good, and her numerous productions (a few excepted) are disfigured by florid ornament and elaborate magnificence."

After Miss Seward's death, in 1809, there was published a small volume with the title of "The Beauties of Anna Seward." She died a maiden. The portrait preceding this brief memoir is a carefully drawn copy with pen and ink of an engraving by A. Carden, from the original picture painted in 1763, when she was sixteen years of age, by Tilly Kettle, an English portrait-painter of note, who was then only about twenty-three years of age.

MONODAY

ON

· MAJOR ANDRÉ.

By Miss SEWARD,

(AUTHOR OF THE ELEGY ON CAPTAIN COOK.)

TO WHICH ARE ADDED

LETTERS ADDRESSED TO HER

By MAJOR ANDRÉ,

IN THE YEAR 1769.

LICHFIELD:

PRINTED AND SOLD BY J. JACKSON, FOR THE AUTHOR ;
SOLD ALSO BY ROBINSON, PATER-NOSTER ROW ; CADELL AND EVANS, IN THE
STRAND, LONDON ; PRINCE, OXFORD ; MERRILL, CAMBRIDGE ;
AND PRATT AND CLINCH, BATH.
M.DCC.LXXXI.

[Price, Two-Shillings-and-Six-Pence.]
10

TO

HIS EXCELLENCY,

SIR HENRY CLINTON,

KNIGHT OF THE BATH.

SIR: *With the zeal of a religious Enthusiast to his murdered Saint, the Author of this mournful Eulogium consecrates it to the Memory of Major André, who fell a Martyr in the Cause of his King and Country, with the firm Intrepidity of a Roman, and the amiable Resignation of a Christian Hero.*

Distant Awe and Reverence prevent her offering these Effusions of Gratitude to the Beneficent and Royal Patron of the André Family. May Mr. André's illustrious General, the Guardian of his injured Honour, his conspicuous and personal Friend, deign to accept them from One who was once happy in the Friendship of the GLORIOUS SUFFERER.

Your Excellency's

Most obedient humble Servant,

ANNA SEWARD.

MONODAY

MAJOR ANDRÉ.

LOUD howls the storm ! the vex'd Atlantic roars !
Thy Genius, Britain, wanders on its shores !
Hears cries of horror, wafted from afar,
And groans of Anguish, mid the shrieks of War !
Hears the deep curses of the Great and Brave,
Sigh in the wind, and murmur on the wave !
O'er his damp brow the sable crape he binds,
And throws his victor-garland * to the winds ;
Bids haggard Winter, in her drear sojourn,
Tear the dim foliage from her drizzling urn ;
With sickly yew unfragrant cypress twine,
And hang the dusky wreath round Honour's shrine.
Bids steel-clad valour chace his dove-like Bride,
Enfeebling Mercy, from his awful side ;
Where long she sat, and check'd the ardent rein,
As whirl'd his chariot o'er th' embattled plain ;
Gilded with sunny smile her April tear,
Rais'd her white arm and stay'd th' uplifted spear ;
Then, in her place, bid Vengeance mount the car,
And glut with gore th' insatiate Dogs of War !—

---

* Victor-garland—alluding to the conquest by Lord Cornwallis.

With one pale hand the bloody scroll * he rears,
And bids his nations blot it with their tears ;
And one, extended o'er th' Atlantic wave,
Points to his ANDRÉ'S ignominious grave !

And shall the Muse, that marks the solemn scene,
" As busy Fancy lifts the veil between,"
Refuse to mingle in the awful train,
Nor breathe with glowing zeal the votive strain ?
From public fame shall admiration fire
The boldest numbers of her ráptur'd lyre
To hymn a Stranger ?—and with ardent lay
Lead the wild mourner round her COOK'S morai,
While ANDRÉ fades upon his dreary bier,
And JULIA'S † only tribute is her tear ?
Dear, lovely Youth ! whose gentle virtues stole
Thro' Friendship's soft'ning medium on her soul !
Ah no !—with every strong resistless plea,
Rise the recorded days she pass'd with thee,
While each dim shadow of o'erwhelming years,
With Eagle-glance reverted, Mem'ry clears.

Belov'd companion of the fairest hours
That rose for her in joy's resplendent bow'rs,
How gaily shone on thy bright Morn of Youth
The Star of Pleasure, and the Sun of Truth !
Full from their Source descended on thy mind
Each gen'rous virtue, and each taste refin'd.

---

* Bloody scroll.   The court-martial decree, signed at Tappan, for Major André's execution.

   † *Julia*—the name by which Mr. André addressed the author in his correspondence with her.

Young Genius led thee to his varied fane,
Bade thee ask *all his gifts, nor ask in vain ;
Hence novel thoughts, in ev'ry lustre drest
Of pointed wit, that diamond of the breast :
Hence glow'd thy fancy with poetic ray,
Hence music warbled in thy sprightly lay ;
And hence thy pencil, with his colours warm,
Caught ev'ry grace, and copied ev'ry charm,
Whose transient glories beam on Beauty's cheek,
And bid the glowing Ivory breathe and speak.
Blest pencil ! by kind Fate ordain'd to save
HONORA's semblance from †her early grave,
Oh ! while on ‡ JULIA's arm it sweetly smiles,
And each lorn thought, each long regret beguiles,
Fondly she weeps the hand, which form'd the spell,
Now shroudless mould'ring in its earthy cell !

But sure the Youth, whose ill-starr'd passion strove
With all the pangs of inauspicious Love,
Full oft' deplor'd the Fatal Art, that stole
The jocund freedom of its Master's soul !

---

* *All his gifts.*—Mr. André has conspicuous talents for Poetry, Music, and Painting. The news-papers mentioned a satiric poem of his upon Americans, which was supposed to have stimulated this barbarity towards him [" The Cow-Chase "].—Of his wit and vivacity, the letters subjoined to this work afford ample proof.—They were addressed to the author by Mr. André when he was a youth of eighteen.

† *Early grave.*—Miss Honora S. [Honora Sneyd], to whom Mr. André's attachment was of such singular constancy, died in a consumption a few months before he suffer'd death at Tappan. She had married another Gentleman [Richard Lovell Edgeworth] four years after her engagement with Mr. André had been dissolved by parental authority.

‡ *Julia's arm.*—Mr. André drew two miniature pictures of Miss Honora S. on his first acquaintance with her at Buxton, in the year 1769, one for himself, the other for the author of this poem.

While with nice hand he mark'd the living grace,
And matchless sweetness of HONORA's face,
Th' enamour'd Youth the faithful traces blest,
That barb'd the dart of Beauty in his breast ;
Around his neck th' enchanting Portrait hung,
While a warm vow burst ardent from his tongue,
That from his bosom no succeeding day,
No chance should bear that Talisman away.
'Twas thus *Apelles bask'd in Beauty's blaze,
And felt the mischief of the steadfast gaze ;
Trac'd with disorder'd hand Campaspe's charms,
And as their beams the kindling Canvas warms,
Triumphant Love, with still superior art,
Engraves their wonders on the Painter's heart.

Dear lost Companion ! ever-constant Youth !
That Fate had smil'd propitious on thy Truth !
Nor bound th' ensanguin'd laurel on that brow
Where Love ordain'd his brightest wreath to glow !
Then Peace had led thee to her softest bow'rs,
And Hymen strew'd thy path with all his flow'rs ;
Drawn to thy roof, by Friendship's silver cord,
Each social Joy had brighten'd at thy board ;
Science, and soft Affection's blended rays
Had shone unclouded on thy lengthen'd days ;
From hour to hour thy taste, with conscious pride,
Had mark'd new talents in thy lovely Bride ;
Till thou hadst own'd the magic of her face
Thy fair HONORA's least engaging grace.

---

* *'Twas thus Apelles.*—Prior is very elegant upon this circumstance in an Ode
to his Friend, Mr. Howard the Painter.

Dear lost HONORA ! o'er thy early bier
Sorrowing the Muse still sheds her sacred tear !
The blushing Rose-bud in its vernal bed,
By Zephyrs fann'd, by glist'ring Dew-drops fed,
In June's gay morn that scents the ambient air,
Was not more sweet, more innocent or fair.
Oh ! when such Pairs their kindred Spirit find,
When Sense and Virtue deck each spotless Mind,
Hard is the doom that shall the union break,
And Fate's dark billow rises o'er the wreck.

Now Prudence, in her cold·and thrifty care,
Frown'd on the Maid, and bade the Youth despair,
For Pow'r Parental sternly saw, and strove
To tear the lily-bands of plighted love ;
Nor strove in vain ;—but while the Fair-One's sighs
Disperse, like April storms in sunny skies,
The firmer Lover, with unswerving truth,
To his first passion consecrates his Youth ;
Tho' four long years a night of absence prove,
Yet Hope's soft Star shone trembling on his Love ;
Till * hov'ring Rumour chas'd the pleasing dream
And veil'd with Raven-wing the silver beam.
" HONORA lost ! my happy Rival's Bride !
" Swell ye full Sails ! and roll thou mighty Tide !
" O'er the dark Waves forsaken ANDRÉ bear
" Amid the vollying Thunders of the War !
" To win bright Glory from my Country's foes,
" E'en in this ice of Love, my bosom glows.

---

* *Hov'ring Rumour.*—The tidings of Honora's Marriage. Upon that event
Mr. André quitted his Profession as a Merchant and join'd our Army in
America.

" Voluptuous LONDON ! in whose gorgeous bow'rs
" The frolic Pleasures lead the dancing Hours,
" From Orient-vales Sabean-odours bring,
" Nor ask her roses of the tardy Spring ;
" Where Paintings burn the Grecian Meed to claim
" From the high Temple of immortal Fame,
" Bears to the radiant Goal, with ardent pace,
" Her Kauffman's Beauty, and her Reynolds' Grace ;
" Where Music floats the glitt'ring roofs among,
" And with meand'ring cadence swells the Song,
" While sun-clad.Poesy the Bard inspires,
" And foils the Grecian Harps, the Latian Lyres.

" Ye soft'ning Luxuries ! ye polish'd Arts !
" Bend your enfeebling rays on tranquil Hearts !
" I quit the Song, the Pencil, and the Lyre,
" White robes of Peace, and Pleasure's soft Attire,
" To seize the Sword, to mount the rapid Car,
" In all the proud habiliments of War.—
" HONORA lost ! I woo a sterner Bride,
" The arm'd Bellona calls me to her side ;
" Harsh is the music of our marriage strain !
" It breathes in thunder from the Western plain !
" Wide o'er the wat'ry world its echoes roll,
" And rouse each latent ardour of my soul.
" And tho' unlike the soft melodious lay,
" That gaily wak'd HONORA's nuptial day,
" Its deeper tones shall whisper, e'er they cease,
" More genuine transport, and more lasting peace !

" Resolv'd I go !—nor from that fatal bourne
" To these gay scenes shall ANDRÉ's step return !

" Set is the Star of Love, that ought to guide
" His refluent Bark across the mighty Tide !—
" But while my Country's Foes, with impious hand,
" Hurl o'er the blasted plains the livid brand
" Of dire Sedition !—Oh ! let Heav'n ordain,
" While ANDRÉ lives, he may not live in vain !

" Yet without one kind farewell, could I roam
" Far from my weeping Friends, my peaceful home,
" The best affections of my heart must cease,
" And gratitude be lost, with hope, and peace !
" My lovely Sisters ! who were wont to twine
" Your Souls' soft feeling with each wish of mine,
" Shall, when this breast beats high at Glory's call,
" From your mild eyes the show'rs of Sorrow fall ?—
"The light of Excellence, that round you glows,
" Decks with reflected beam your Brother's brows.
" Oh ! may his Fame, in some distinguish'd day,
" Pour on that Excellence the brightest ray !
" Dim clouds of woe ! ye veil each sprightly grace
" That us'd to sparkle in MARIA'S face.—
" My *tuneful ANNA to her lute complains,
" But Grief's fond throbs arrest the parting strains.—
" Fair as the silver blossom on the thorn,
" Soft as the spirit of the vernal morn,
" LOUISA, chace those trembling fears, that prove
" Th' ungovern'd terrors of a Sister's love.
" They bend thy sweet head, like yon lucid flow'r,
" That shrinks and fades beneath the summer's show'r—
" Oh ! smile, my Sisters, on this destin'd day,

---

* *Tuneful Anna.*—Miss Anna André has a poetical talent.

" And with the radiant omen gild my way.!
" And thou, my Brother, gentle as the gale,
" Whose breath perfumes anew the blossom'd vale,
" Yet quick of Spirit, as th' electric beam,
" When from the clouds its darting lightnings stream,
" Soothe with incessant care our Mother's woes,
" And hush her anxious sighs to soft repose.—
" And be ye sure, when distant far I stray
" To share the dangers of the arduous day,
" Your tender faithful amity shall rest
" The * last dear record of my grateful breast.

" Oh ! graceful Priestess at the fane of Truth,
" Friend of my Soul ! and Guardian of my Youth !
" Skill'd to convert the duty to the choice,
" My gentle Mother !—in whose melting voice
" The virtuous precept, that perpetual flow'd,
" With music warbled, and with beauty glow'd,
" Thy Tears !—ah Heav'n !—not drops of molten lead,
" Pour'd on thy hapless Son's devoted head,
" With keener smart had each sensation torn !—
" They wake the nerve where agonies are born !
" But oh ! restrain me not !—thy tender strife,
" What wou'd it save ?—alas !—thy ANDRÉ'S life !
" Oh ! what a weary pilgrimage 'twill prove
" Strew'd with the thorns of disappointed Love !
" Ne'er can he break the charm, whose fond controul,
" By habit rooted, lords it o'er his soul,

---

* *Last dear record.*—" I have a Mother, and three Sisters, to whom the value
" of my commission wou'd be an object, as the loss of Grenada has much affected
" their income. It is needless to be more explicit on this subject, I know your Ex-
" cellency's goodness."—See Major André's last letter to General Clinton, publish'd
in the Gazette.

" If here he languish in inglorious ease,
" Where Science palls, and Pleasures cease to please.
" 'Tis Glory only, with her potent ray,
' Can chace the clouds that darken all his way.
" Then dry those pearly drops that wildly flow,
" Nor snatch the laurel from my youthful brow !—
" The Rebel Standard blazes to the noon !
" And Glory's path is bright before thy Son !
" Then join thy voice ! and thou with Heav'n ordain
" While ANDRÉ lives, he may not live in vain ! "

He says !—and sighing seeks the busy strand,
Where anchor'd Navies wait the wish'd command.
To the full gale the nearer billows roar,
And proudly lash the circumscribing shore ;
While furious on the craggy coast they rave,
All calm and lovely rolls the distant wave ;
For onward, as th' unbounded waters spread,
Deep sink the rocks in their capacious bed,
And all their pointed terror's utmost force
But gently interrupts the billow's course.

So on his present hour rude Passion preys !
So smooth the prospect of his future days !
Unconscious of the Storm, that grimly sleeps,
To wreck its fury on th' unshelter'd Deeps !
Now yielding Waves divide before the prow,
The white sails bend, the streaming pennants glow ;
And swiftly waft him to the Western plain,
Where fierce Bellona rages o'er the slain.

Firm in their strength, opposing Legions stand,
Prepar'd to drench with blood the thirsty Land.

Now Carnage hurls her flaming bolts afar,
And Desolation groans amid the War.
As bleed the Valiant, and the Mighty yield,
Death stalks, the only Victor, o'er the field.

Foremost in all the horrors of the day,
Impetuous ANDRÉ * leads the glorious way ;
Till, rashly bold, by numbers forc'd to yield,
They drag him captive from the long-fought field.—
Around the Hero crowd th' exulting Bands,
And seize the spoils of war with bloody hands,
Snatch the dark plumage from his awful crest,
And tear the golden crescent from his breast ;
The sword, the tube, that wings the death from far,
And all the fatal implements of War !

Silent, unmov'd the gallant Youth survey'd
The lavish spoils triumphant Ruffians made.
The idle ornament, the useless spear
He little recks, but oh ! there is a fear
Pants with quick throb, while yearning sorrows dart
Thro' his chill frame, and tremble at his heart :

" What tho' HONORA'S voice no more shall charm !
" No more her beamy smile my bosom warm !
" Yet from these eyes shall force for ever tear
" The sacred Image of that Form so dear ?—
" Shade of my Love ! †—tho' mute and cold thy charms,
" Ne'er hast thou blest my happy Rival's arms !

---

* *Impetuous André.*—It is in this passage only that fiction has been employ'd
thro' the narrative of the poem. Mr. André was a prisoner in America, soon after
his arrival there, but the Author is unacquainted with the circumstances of the
action in which he was taken.
†*Shade of my Love.*—The miniature of Honora. A letter from Major André

" To my sad heart each Dawn has seen thee prest !
" Each Night has laid thee pillow'd on my breast !
" Force shall not tear thee from thy faithful shrine ;
" Shade of my Love ! thou shalt be ever mine !

" 'Tis fix'd !—these lips shall resolute enclose
" The precious Soother of my ceaseless woes.
" And shou'd relentless Violence invade
" This last retreat, by frantic Fondness made,
" One way remains !—Fate whispers to my Soul
" Intrepid * Portia and her burning coal !
" So shall the throbbing Inmate of my breast
" From Love's sole gift meet everlasting rest ! "

While these sad thoughts in swift succession fire
The smother'd embers of each fond desire,
Quick to his mouth his eager hands removes
The beauteous semblance of the Form he loves.
That darling treasure safe, resign'd he wears
The sordid robe, the scanty viand shares ;
With cheerful fortitude content to wait
The barter'd ransom of a kinder Fate.

Now many a Moon in her pale course had shed
The pensive beam on ANDRÉ'S captive head.

---

to one of his Friends, written a few years ago, contained the following sentence :
" I have been taken prisoner by the Americans and stript of everything except the
" picture of Honora, which I concealed in my mouth. Preserving that, I yet think
" myself fortunate."

    * *Intrepid Portia.*—" *Brutus*]. Impatient of my absence,
           " And grieved that young Octavius with Mark Antony
           " Had made themselves so strong, she grew distracted,
           " And, her Attendants absent, swallow'd fire.
           " *Cassius.*] And dy'd so ?
           " *Brutus.*] Even so ! "
See Shakespear's Play of Julius Cæsar, Act IV., Scene IV.

At length the Sun rose jocund, to adorn
With all his splendour the enfranchis'd Morn.
Again the Hero joins the ardent Train
That pours its thousands on the tented plain ;
And shines distinguish'd in the long Array,
Bright as the silver Star that leads the Day !
His modest temperance, his wakeful heed,
His silent diligence, his ardent speed,
Each Warrior-duty to the Veteran taught,
Shaming the vain Experience Time had brought.
Dependence scarcely feels his gentle sway,
He shares each want, and smiles each grief away ;
And to the virtues of a noble Heart,
Unites the talents of inventive Art.
Thus from his swift and faithful pencil flow
The Lines, the Camp, the Fortress of the Foe ;
Serene to counteract each deep design,
Points the dark Ambush, and the springing Mine ;
Till, as a breathing Incense, ANDRÉ'S name
Pervades the Host, and swells the loud acclaim.

The CHIEF no virtue views with cold regard,
Skill'd to discern, and generous to reward ;
Each tow'ring hope his honour'd smiles impart,
As near his Person, and more near his Heart
The graceful Youth he draws,—and round his brow
Bids Rank and Pow'r their mingled brilliance throw.

Oh ! hast thou seen a blooming Morn of May
In crystal beauty shed the modest ray,
And with its balmy dews' refreshing show'r
Swell the young grain, and ope the purple flow'r,

In bright'ning lustre reach its radiant Noon,
Rob'd in the gayest mantle of the Sun?
Then 'mid the splendours of its azure skies,
Oh! hast thou seen the cruel Storm arise,
In sable horror shroud each dazzling charm,
And dash their glories back with icy arm?

Thus lowr'd the deathful cloud amid the blaze
Of ANDRÉ'S rising hopes,—and quench'd their rays!
Ah, fatal Embassy!—thy hazards dire
His kindling Soul with ev'ry ardour fire;
Great CLINTON gives it to the courage prov'd,
And the known wisdom of the Friend he lov'd.

As fair Euryalus, to meet his Fate,
With Nysus rushes from the Dardan gate,
Relentless Fate! whose fury scorns to spare
The snowy breast, red lip, and shining hair,
So polish'd ANDRÉ launches on the waves,
Where * Hudson's tide its dreary confine laves.
With firm intrepid foot the Youth explores
Each dangerous pathway of the hostile shores;
But on no Veteran-Chief his step attends,
As silent round the gloomy Wood he wends;
Alone he meets the brave repentant Foe,
Sustains his late resolve, receives his vow,
With ardent skill directs the doubtful course,
Seals the firm bond, and ratifies its force.
'Tis thus, AMERICA, thy Generals fly,
And wave new banners in their native sky!

---

* *Hudson's tide.*—Major André came up the Hudson River to meet General
Arnold.   On his return by Land he fell into the hands of the Enemy.

Sick of the mischiefs artful GALLIA pours,
In friendly semblance on thy ravag'd shores.
Unnatural compact !—shall a Race of Slaves
Sustain the ponderous standard Freedom waves ?
No ! while their feign'd Protection spreads the toils,
The Vultures hover o'er the destin'd spoils !
How fade Provincial-glories, while ye run
To court far deeper bondage than ye shun !
Is this the generous active rising Flame,
That boasted Liberty's immortal name,
Blaz'd for its rights infring'd, its trophies torn,
And taught the Wife the dire mistake to mourn,
When haughty BRITAIN, in a luckless hour,
With rage inebriate, and the lust of pow'r,
To fruitless conquest, and to countless graves,
Led her gay Legions o'er the Western waves ?
The Friend of Discord, cow'ring at the prow,
Sat darkly smiling at th' impending woe !

Long did my Soul the wretched strife survey,
And wept the horrors of the deathful day ;
Thro' rolling Years saw undecisive War
Drag bleeding Wisdom at his iron Car ;
Exhaust my Country's treasure, pour her gore
In fruitless conflict on the distant shore ;
Saw the firm CONGRESS all her might oppose,
And while I mourn'd her fate, rever'd her Foes.

But when, repentant of her prouder aim,
She gently waives the long-disputed claim ;
Extends the Charter with your Rights restor'd,
And hides in olive-wreaths the blood-stain'd sword,

Then to reject her peaceful wreaths, and throw
Your Country's Freedom to our mutual Foe !—
Infatuate Land !—from that detested day
Distracted Councils, and the thirst of Sway,
Rapacious Avarice, Superstition vile,
And all the *Frenchman* dictates in his guile
Disgrace your CONGRESS !—Justice drops her scale !
And radiant Liberty averts her sail !
They fly indignant the polluted plain,
Where Truth is scorn'd, and Mercy pleads in vain.
That she does plead in vain, thy witness bear,
Accursed Hour !—thou darkest of the Year !
That with Misfortune's deadliest venom fraught,
To Tappan's Wall the gallant ANDRÉ brought.

Oh WASHINGTON ! I thought thee great and good,
Nor knew thy Nero-thirst of guiltless blood !
Severe to use the pow'r that Fortune gave,
Thou cool determin'd Murderer of the Brave !
Lost to each fairer Virtue, that inspires
The genuine fervor of the patriot fires !
And You, the base Abettors of the doom,
That sunk his blooming honors in the tomb,
Th' opprobrious tomb your harden'd hearts decreed,
While all he ask'd was as the Brave to Bleed !
Nor other boon the glorious Youth implor'd
Save the cold Mercy of the Warrior-Sword !
O dark, and pitiless ! your impious hate
O'er-whelm'd the Hero in the Ruffian's fate !
Stopt with the * Felon-cord the rosy breath !
And venom'd with disgrace the darts of Death !

---

* *Felon-cord.*—" As I suffer in the defence of my Country, I must consider this
" hour as the most glorious of my life.—Remember that I die as becomes a British

Remorseless WASHINGTON ! the day shall come
Of deep repentance for this barb'rous doom !
When injur'd ANDRÉ'S memory shall inspire
A kindling Army with resistless fire :
Each falchion sharpen that the Britons wield,
And lead their fiercest Lion to the field !
Then, when each hope of thine shall set in night,
When dubious dread, and unavailing flight
Impel your Host, thy.guilt-upbraided Soul
Shall wish untouch'd the sacred Life you stole !
And when thy Heart appall'd and vanquish'd Pride
Shall vainly ask the mercy they deny'd,
With horror shalt thou meet the fate they gave,
Nor Pity gild the darkness of thy grave !
For Infamy, with livid hand shall shed
Eternal mildew on the ruthless head !

Less cruel far than thou, on Ilium's plain
Achilles, raging for Patroclus slain !
When hapless Priam bends the aged knee,
To deprecate the Victor's dire decree,
The nobler Greek, in melting pity spares
The lifeless Hector to his Father's prayers,
Fierce as he was ;—'tis *Cowards* only know
Persisting vengeance o'er a *fallen* Foe.

But no intreaty wakes the soft remorse,
Oh, murder'd ANDRÉ ! for thy sacred Corse ;
Vain were an army's, vain its Leader's sighs !—
Damp in the Earth on Hudson's shore it lies !

" Officer, while the manner of my death must reflect disgrace on your Comi
See Major André's last words, inserted in the General Evening Post, for '
November the 14, 1780.

Unshrouded welters in the wintry storm,
And gluts the riot of the * Tappan Worm !
But oh ! its dust, like Abel's blood, shall rise,
And call for justice from the angry skies !

What tho' the Tyrants, with malignant pride,
To thy pale Corse each decent rite deny'd !
Thy graceful limbs in no kind covert laid,
Nor with the Christian Requiem sooth'd thy shade !
Yet on thy grass-green Bier soft April-show'rs
Shall earliest wake the sweet spontaneous Flow'rs,
Bid the blue Hare-bell and the Snow-drop there
Hang their cold cup, and drop the pearly tear !
And oft, at pensive Eve's ambiguous gloom,
Imperial Honour, bending o'er thy tomb,
With solemn strains shall lull thy deep repose,
And with his deathless Laurels shade thy brows !

Lamented Youth ! while with inverted spear
The British Legions pour th' indignant tear !
Round the dropt arm the † funeral scarf entwine,
And in their heart's deep core thy worth enshrine,
While my weak Muse, in fond attempt and vain,
. But feebly pours a perishable strain,
Oh ! ye distinguish'd Few ! whose glowing lays
Bright Phœbus kindles with his purest rays,
Snatch from its radiant source the living fire,
And light with ‡ Vestal flame your ANDRÉ'S HALLOW'D
    PYRE.

---

* *Tappan.*—The place where Major André was executed.

† *Funeral scarf.*—Our whole Army in America went into mourning for Major André, a distinguish'd tribute to his merit.

‡ *Vestal flame.*—The Vestal fire was kept perpetually burning, and originally kindled from the rays of the Sun.

LETTERS

ADDRESSED TO THE AUTHOR OF THE FOREGOING POEM, BY MAJOR
ANDRÉ, WHEN HE WAS A YOUTH OF EIGHTEEN.

LETTER I.

CLAPTON, *October 3, 1769.*

FROM their agreeable excursion to Shrewsbury, my dear-
est friends are by this time returned to their thrice-beloved
Lichfield. Once again have they beheld those fortunate
spires, the constant witnesses of all their pains and pleasures.
I can well conceive the emotions of joy which their first appearance, from the neighboring hills, excites after absence;
they seem to welcome you home, and invite you to reiterate
those hours of happiness, of which they are a species of
monument. I shall have an eternal love and reverence for
them. Never shall I forget the joy that danced in Honora's
eyes, when she first showed them to me from Needwood
Forest on our return with you from Buxton to Lichfield. I
remember she called them the *Ladies of the Valley*—their
lightness and elegance deserve the title. Oh, how I loved
them from that instant! My enthusiasm concerning them
is carried farther even than yours and Honora's, for every
object that has a pyramidal form recalls them to my recol-
lection, with a sensation that brings the tear of pleasure into
my eyes.

How happy must you have been at Shrewsbury! only that you tell me, alas! that dear Honora was not so well as you wished during your stay there. 1 always hope the best. My impatient spirit rejects every obtruding idea which I have not fortitude to support. Dr. Darwin's skill and your tender care will remove that sad pain in her side, which makes writing troublesome and injurious to her; which robs her poor *cher Jean* * of .those precious pages with which, he flatters himself, she would otherwise have indulged him. So your happiness at Shrewsbury scorned to be indebted to public amusements. Five virgins, united in the soft bonds of friendship! how I should have liked to have made the sixth! But you surprise me by such an absolute exclusion of the beaux. I certainly thought that when five wise virgins were watching at midnight, it must have been in expectation of the bridegroom's coming. *We* are at this instant five virgins, writing round the same table —my three sisters, Mr. Ewer, and myself. I beg no reflections injurious to the honor of poor *cher Jean.* My mother is gone to pay a visit, and has left us in possession of the old coach; but as for nags, we can boast only of two long-tails, and my sisters say they are sorry cattle, being no other than my friend Ewer and myself, who, to say the truth, have enormous pig-tails.

My dear Boissier is come to town; he has brought a little of the soldier with him, but he is the same honest, warm, intelligent friend 1 always found him. He sacrifices the town diversions, since 1 will not partake of them.

We are jealous of your correspondents, who are so numerous. Yet, write to the Andrés often, my dear Julia, for

---

* A name of kindness, by which Mr. André was often called by his mother and sisters, and generally adopted by the persons mentioned in these letters.

who are they that will value your letters quite so much as
we value them ?

The least scrap of a letter will be received with the greatest joy. Write, therefore, though it were only to give us
the comfort of having a piece of paper which has recently
passed through your hands; Honora will put in a little
postscript, were it only to tell me that she is *my very sincere
friend*, who will neither give me love nor comfort—very
short, indeed, Honora, was thy last postscript! But I am
too presumptuous ; I will not scratch out, but I *unsay*.
From the little there *was* I received more joy than I deserve. This *cher Jean* is an impertinent fellow, but he will
grow discreet in time. You must consider him as a poor
novice of *eighteen*, who, for all the sins he may commit, is
sufficiently punished in the single evil of being one hundred
and twenty miles from Lichfield.

My mother and sisters will go to Putney in a few days,
to stay some time. We none of us like Clapton. *I* need not
care, for I am all day long in town, but it is avoiding Scylla
to fall into Charybdis. You paint to me the pleasant vale of
Stow in the richest autumnal coloring. In return, I must tell
you that my zephyrs are wafted through cracks in the wain-
scot; for murmuring streams I have dirty kennels; for bleat-
ing flocks, grunting pigs ; and squalling cats for birds that in-
cessantly warble. I have said something of this sort in my
letter to Miss Spearman, and am twinged with the idea of
these epistles being confronted, and that I shall recall to
your memory the fat knight's love-letters to Mrs. Ford and
Mrs. Page.

Julia, perhaps thou fanciest I am merry—alas ! But I do
not wish to make you as doleful as myself ; and besides,
when I would express the tender feelings of my soul, I have

no language which does them justice ; if I had, I should regret that you could not have it fresher, and that whatever
one communicates by letter must go such a roundabout way
before it reaches one's correspondent — from the writer's
heart, through his head, arm, hand, pen, ink, paper, over
many a weary hill and dale, to the eye, head, and heart of
the reader. I have often regretted our not possessing a
sort of faculty which should enable our sensations, remarks,
etc., to arise from their source in a sort of exaltations, and
fall upon our paper in words and phrases properly adapted
to express them, without passing through an imagination
whose operations so often fail to second those of the heart.
Then what a metamorphose should we see in people's style!
How eloquent those who are truly attached! how stupid
they who falsely profess affection! Perhaps the former had
never been able to express half their regard ; while the latter, by their flowers of rhetoric, had made us believe a thousand times more than they ever felt—but this is whimsical
moralizing.

My sisters Penserosas were dispersed on their arrival
in town, by the joy of seeing Louisa and their dear little
brother Billy again, our kind and excellent Uncle Giradot,
and Uncle Lewis André. I was glad to see them, but they
complained, not without reason, of the gloom upon my
countenance. Billy wept for joy that we were returned,
while poor *cher Jean* was ready to weep for sorrow. Louisa
is grown still handsomer since we left her. Our sisters,
Mary and Anne, knowing your partiality to beauty, are
afraid that, when they introduce her to you, she will put
their noses out of joint. Billy is not old enough for me
to be afraid of in the rival-way, else I should keep him
aloof, for his heart is formed of those affectionate ma-

terials so dear to the ingenuous taste of Julia and her Honora.

. I sympathize in your resentment against the canonical dons who stumpify the heads of those good green* people, beneath whose friendly shade so many of your happiest hours have glided away—but they defy them ; let them stumpify as much as they please, time will repair the mischief ; their verdant arms will again extend and invite you to their shelter.

The evenings grow long. I hope your conversation round the fire will sometimes fall on the Andrés ; it will be a great comfort that they are remembered: We chink our glasses to your healths at every meal. " Here's to our Lichfieldian friends," says Nanny. "Oh-h !" says Mary. " With all my soul, say I." "*Allons !*" cries my mother— and the draught seems nectar. The libation made, we begin our uncloying theme, and so beguile the gloomy evening.

Mr. and Mrs. Seward will accept my most affectionate respects. My male friend at Lichfield will join in your conversation on the Andrés. Among the numerous good qualities he is possessed of, he certainly has gratitude, and then he can not forget those who so sincerely love and esteem him. I, in particular, shall always recall with pleasure the happy hours I have passed in his company. My friendship for him, and for your family, has diffused itself, like the precious ointment from Aaron's beard, on everything which surrounds you ; therefore I beg you would give my amities to the whole town. Persuade Honora to forgive the length and ardor of the enclosed, and believe me truly,

.   Your affectionate and faithful friend,

J. ANDRÉ.

---

* The trees in the cathedral-walk in Lichfield.

LONDON, *October 19, 1769.* ·

FROM the midst of books, papers, bills, and other implements of gain, let me lift up my drowsy head awhile to con-
verse with dear Julia. And first, as I know she has a fervent
wish to see me a quill-driver, I must tell her that I begin, as
people are wont to do, to look upon my future profession
with great partiality. I no longer see it in so disadvan-
tageous a light. Instead of figuring a merchant as a middle-
aged man, with a bob-wig, a rough beard, in snuff-colored
clothes, grasping a guinea in his red hand, I conceive a come-
ly young man, with a tolerable pig-tail, wielding a pen with
all the noble fierceness of the Duke of Marlborough brandish-
ing a truncheon upon a sign-post, surrounded with types
and emblems, and canopied with cornucopias that disem-
bogue their stores upon his head ; Mercuries reclined upon
bales of goods ; Genii playing with pens, ink, and paper ;
while in perspective, his gorgeous vessels, "launched on the
bosom of the silver Thames," are wafting to distant lands
the produce of this commercial nation. Thus all the mercantile glories crowd on my fancy, emblazoned in the most
refulgent coloring of an ardent imagination. Borne on her
soaring pinions, I wing my flight to the time when Heaven
shall have crowned my labors with success and opulence. I
see sumptuous palaces rising to receive me. I see orphans,
and widows, and painters, and fiddlers, and poets, and build-
ers, protected and encouraged ; and when the fabric is pretty
nearly finished by my shattered pericranium, I cast my eyes
around and find John André by a small coal-fire, in a gloomy
compting-house in Warnford Court, nothing so little as what
he has been making himself, and in all probability never to

be much more than he is at present. But oh, my dear Honora! it is for thy sake only I wish for wealth. You say she was somewhat better at the time you wrote last. I must flatter myself that she will soon be without any remains of this threatening disease.

It is seven o'clock. You and Honora, with two or three more select friends, are now probably encircling your dressing-room fireplace. What would I not give to enlarge that circle! The idea of a clean hearth, and a snug circle round it, formed by a few sincere friends, transports me. You seem combined together against the inclemency of the weather, the hurry, bustle, ceremony, censoriousness, and envy of the world. The purity, the warmth, the kindly influence of fire, to all for whom it is kindled, is a good emblem of the friendship of such amiable minds as Julia's and her Honora's. Since I can not be there in reality, pray imagine me with you ; admit me to your *conversaziones ;* think how I wish for the blessing of joining them !—and be persuaded that I take part in all your pleasures, in the dear hope that e'er it be very long your blazing hearth will burn again for me. Pray keep me a place ; let the poker, tongs, or shovel, represent me ; but you have Dutch tiles, which are infinitely better ; so let Moses, or Aaron, or Balaam's ass, be my representative.

But time calls me to Clapton. I quit you abruptly till to-morrow, when, if I do not tear the nonsense I have been writing, I may perhaps increase its quantity. Signora Cynthia is in clouded majesty. Silvered with her beams, I am about to jog to Clapton upon my own stumps ; musing as I homeward plod my way—ah ! need I name the subject of my contemplations ?

I had a sweet walk home last night, and found the Clap-tonians, with their fair guest, a Miss Mourgue, very well. My sisters send their *amitiés*, and will write in a few days.

This morning I returned to town. It has been the finest day imaginable. A solemn mildness was diffused throughout the blue horizon ; its light was clear and distinct rather than dazzling. The serene beams of the autumnal sun, gilded hills, variegated woods, glittering spires, ruminating herds, bounding flocks, all combined to enchant the eyes, expand the heart, and

> " Chace all sorrow but despair."

In the midst of such a scene no lesser grief can prevent our sympathy with Nature. A calmness, a benevolent disposition seizes us with sweet, insinuating power. The very brute creation seems sensible of these beauties ; there is a species of mild cheerfulness in the face of a lamb which I have but indifferently expressed in a corner of my paper, and a demure, contented look in an ox, which, in the fear of expressing still worse, I leave unattempted.

Business calls me away. I must dispatch my letter. Yet what does it contain ?—no matter. You like anything better than news. Indeed, you never told me so ; but I have an intuitive knowledge upon the subject, from the sympathy which I have constantly perceived in the taste of Julia and *cher Jean*. What is it to you or me—

> If here in the city we have nothing but riot,
> If the Spital-field weavers can't be kept quiet,
> If the weather is fine, or the streets should be dirty,
> Or if Mr. Dick Wilson died aged of thirty ?

But if I was to hearken to the versifying grumbling I feel within me, I should fill my paper and not have room left to

entreat that you would plead my cause to Honora more elo-
quently than the enclosed letter has the power of doing.
Apropos of verses, you desire me to recollect my random
description of the engaging appearance of the charming
Mrs. ——. Here it is, at your service :

> Then rustling and bustling the lady comes down,
> With a flaming red face, and a broad yellow gown,
> And a hobbling out-of-breath gait, and a frown.

This little French cousin of ours, Delarise, was my sister
Mary's playfellow at Paris. His sprightliness engages my
sisters extremely. Doubtless they talk much of him to you
in their letters. How sorry I am to bid you adieu ! Oh, let
me not be forgot by the friends' most dear to you at Lichfield ! *Lichfield !* Ah ! of what magic letters is that little
word composed ! How graceful it looks when it is written !
Let nobody talk to me of its original meaning, * " The field
of blood ! " Oh, no such thing ! It is the field of joy !
" The beautiful city that lifts her fair head in the valley and
says, I *am*, and there is none beside me ! " Who says she is
vain ? Julia will not say so, nor yet Honora, and least of all
their devoted   J. ANDRE.

<hr>

LETTER III.

CLAPTON, *November 1, 1769.*

MY ears still ring with the sounds of "O Jack ! O Jack !
How do the dear Lichfieldians ? What do they say ? What

<hr>

* *Field of blood.*—Here is a small mistake. Lichfield is not the field of blood,
but "the field of dead bodies," alluding to the battle fought between the Romans
and the British Christians in the Diocletian persecution, when the latter were mas-
sacred. Three slain kings, with their burying-place, now Barrowcop Hill, and the
cathedral in miniature, form the city arms. Lich is still a word in use. The
churchyard gates, through which funerals pass, are often called Lich-gates, vul-
garly Light-gates.

are they about? What did *you* do while you were with them?" Have patience, said I, good people! and began my story, which they devoured with as, much joyful avidity as Adam did Gabriel's tidings of heaven. My mother and sisters are all very well, and delighted with their little Frenchman, who is a very agreeable lad. Surely you applaud the fortitude with which I left you! Did I not come off with flying colors? It was a great effort, for, alas! this recreant heart did *not second* the smiling courage of the *countenance ;* nor is it yet as it ought to be, from the hopes that it may reasonably entertain of seeing you all again e'er the winter's dreary hours are past. Julia, my dear Julia, gild them with tidings of our beloved Honora! Oh, that you may be able to tell me that she regains her health, and her charming vivacity! Your sympathizing heart partakes all the joys and pains of your friends. Never can I forget its kind offices, which were of such moment to my peace! *Mine* is formed for friendship, and I am blessed in being able to place so *well* the purest passion of an ingenuous mind! How am I honored in Mr. and Mrs. Seward's attachment to me! Charming were the anticipations which beguiled the long tracts of hill, and dale, and plain that divide London from Lichfield! With what delight my eager eyes *drank* their first view of the dear spires! What rapture did I not feel on entering your gates! in flying up the hall steps! in rushing into the dining-room! in meeting the gladdened eyes of dear Julia and her enchanting friend! That instant convinced me of the truth of Rousseau's observation, that "there are *moments* worth ages." Shall not those moments return? Ah, Julia! the cold hand of absence is heavy upon the heart of your poor *cher Jean.* He is forced to hammer into it perpetually every consoling argument that the magic wand of hope can conjure up, viz., that every moment of industrious absence advances his journey, you know whither. I may sometimes make excursions to Lichfield, and bask in the light of my Honora's eyes! Sustain me, Hope!—nothing on my part shall be wanting which may induce thee to *fulfill* thy blossoming promises.

The happy social circle—Julia, Honora, Miss S——n, Miss B——n, her brother, Mr. S——e, Mr. R——n, etc., etc.— are now, perhaps, enlivening your dressing-room, the dear *blue region*, as Honora calls it, with the sensible observation; the tasteful criticism, or the elegant song; dreading the iron-tongue of the nine-o'clock bell, which disperses the beings whom friendship and kindred virtues had drawn together. My imagination attaches itself to *all*, even the *inanimate* objects which surround Honora and her Julia; that have beheld their graces and virtues expand and ripen—my dear Honora's—from their infant bud.

The sleepy Claptonian train are gone to bed, somewhat wearied with their excursion to Enfield, whither they have this day carried their favorite little Frenchman, so *great* a favorite; the parting was quite tragical. I walked hither from town, as usual, to-night; no hour of the twenty-four is so precious to me as that devoted to this solitary walk. O my friend! I am far from possessing the patient frame of mind which I so continually invoke! Why is Lichfield an hundred and twenty miles from me? There is no *moderation* in the distance! Fifty or sixty miles had been a great deal too much, but *then* there would have been less opposition from *authority* to my frequent visits. I conjure you, supply the want of these blessings by frequent *letters*. I must not, will not ask them of Honora, since the use of the pen is forbid to her declining health; I will content myself, as usual, with a postscript from her in your epistle. My sisters are charmed with the packet which arrived yesterday, and which they will answer soon.

As yet I have said nothing of our journey. We met an entertaining Irish gentleman at Dunchurch, and, being fellow-sufferers in cold and hunger, joined interests, ordered four horses, and stuffed three in a chaise. It is not to *you* —I need not apologize for talking in rapture of an higgler whom we met on our road. His cart had passed us, and was at a considerable distance, when, looking back, he perceived that our chaise had stopped, and that the driver seemed mending something. He ran up to him, and with a face full of honest anxiety, pity, good-nature, and every sweet affection under heaven, asked him if we wanted anything ; that he had plenty of nails, ropes, etc., in his cart. That wretch of a postillion made no other reply than " We want nothing, master." From the same impulse the good Irishman, Mr. Till, and myself, thrust our heads instantly out of the chaise, and tried to recompense to the honest creature by forcing upon him a little pecuniary tribute. My benevolence will be the warmer, while I live, for the treasured remembrance of this higgler's countenance.

I know you interest yourself in my destiny. I have now completely subdued my aversion to the profession of a merchant, and hope in time to acquire an inclination for it ; yet God forbid I should ever love what I am to make the object of my attention !—that vile trash, which I care not for, but only as it may be the future means of procuring the blessing of my soul. Thus all my mercantile calculations go to the tune of *dear Honora*. When an impertinent consciousness whispers in my ear that I am not of the right stuff for a merchant, I draw my Honora's picture from my bosom, and

12

the sight of that dear talisman so inspirits my industry that no toil appears oppressive.

The poetic talk you set me in is a sad method. My head and heart are too full of other matters to be engrossed by a draggle-tailed wench of the Heliconian puddle. I am going to try my interest in Parliament. How you stare!—it is to procure a frank. Be so good as to give the enclosed to Honora ; *it* will speak to *her.* And do *you* say everything that is kind for me to every *other* distinguished friend of the dressing-room circle ; encourage them in their obliging desire of scribbling in your letters, but don't let them take Honora's corner of the sheet.

Adieu ! May you all possess that cheerfulness denied to your *cher Jean.* I fear it hurts my mother to see my musing moods, but I can neither help nor overcome them. The near hopes of another excursion to Lichfield could alone disperse every gloomy vapor of my imagination. Again, and yet again, adieu !

J. ANDRÉ.

INDEX.

THE END.